BEWARE 30!

by

Jacy M. Wade

BEWARE 30!

This book is dedicated to:

My mother, *Ethel M Wagner*, **for always telling me I could do anything I put my heart into.**

And

My father, *John M Wagner*, **for always telling me to Just Do It, stop thinking about it and Just Do It!**

I wish to say thank you for all the support I received from my family. My husband: John for his medical and military knowledge, as well as his patience and encouragement; my son Jeremy for his fire-rescue experience and techniques; my daughter Jenifer the worlds best editor for a new author, without her help and careful proofreading this novel would have been a readers nightmare.

I could not have completed this project without their love and help. MY LOVE AND THANKS TO ALL OF YOU!

A special thanks to Kelly for her initial editing help, she got me started.

Chapter 1

Tuesday
11 Sept '07

She awoke slowly to the sounds of the little ones sleeping, knowing the sun was just beginning its rise. The arm around her slowly tightened as Black Hawk whispered, "Morning, my little Wolf, what do you wish on your birthing day?"

Smiling, she turned to face her lover, her soul mate, her reason for being, and gently kissed him. "This is all I want, to be like this forever."

"That would spoil the kits' surprises, but if you wish..." and laughing quietly, he rolled to her and started her morning with the softest kiss. Slowly it grew stronger, as his hands lightly caressed her ear lobes and teased her neck. Trailing kisses across her chin and cheek, he began nibbling on a sensitive lobe, and licking the lovely spot right behind it. Lilac Wolf stretched her body so it was lined up better with his, and gave a bit of a purr.

Jade wakes smiling, and reaches for Jake...only to find the empty bed. Looking at the alarm clock she grumbles, "He's already in the shower. Damn, I could use a bit of that morning wake-up myself. Well, time to get up and get the day started. Kids to get off to school, work to get to." She looks at the clock again. "Hmmm...I've still got 15 minutes, maybe he needs help washing his back?" Quickly she undresses and enters the steamy master bathroom.

9

Forty-five minutes later, the children are waiting for the bus, Jake is on his way to teach his classes at the Navy Academy, and Jade is almost ready for work. "I should have more dreams like that!" she says to herself, with a slight shiver of delight. "What a great way to start the day." She takes one last look in the mirror. Everything's in place, no smudges on her face, the light mauve eyeliner on her lids is perfect for a change. No spots on her clothes, she didn't smear any powered foundation on her top this time. She's ready to go.

Jade stops and really looks at herself for a change She's of average height, 5'6" and average weight, 135 lbs; Her hair is medium brown with so much red it's almost auburn, loosely shagged to her shoulders. Her eyes are blue, even if one tends to turn green depending on what she's wearing. She's kind of cute, but no great beauty, just a nice average 30-year-old married, mother of twins. At least that's how she sees herself. Jake sees someone entirely different and Jade isn't going to complain a whole lot about that.

Entering the back door of the Three Sisters Travel Agency with a dreamy look on her face, Jade drops her purse on her desk and walks into the back office to start the coffee. While it's perking, she reads over the night's faxes to check out the latest specials. Currently she's working on two honeymoons, three cruises, and a Disney package. It's always a good idea to check and see if any better offers have come in.

Filling her mug, she moves back to her desk and starts up the computer. She has fifteen or twenty minutes before anyone else will arrive. This is her time to get organized. She needs these few minutes of quiet to get into "Super Travel Agent" mode. It's what makes her so good at her job, helps her focus on what she does, and allows her to keep so many accounts straight at once. Soon enough the Sisters will come in and the front door will open. Jade scans over the files, double-checks that everything is up to date, makes her daily to-do list, sips her coffee, and smiles smugly. This is going to be a *very* good day!

She really enjoys being a travel agent, and Jade's good at it. She loves puzzles and that's what putting together a vacation package is. You take a variety of information from your clients, mix it with information you receive from your suppliers, on the Internet and/or personal experience, shake well, and end up with the right holiday for the right person. Jake says it's more of an art than a science and she can't really disagree.

Her favorite part of being an agent is the familiarization trips. The chance to experience the resorts or cruise ships that she is selling, usually at a very reduced rate. Once upon a time, the travel agent could travel for free, or damn near, but not any more. The economy just is not that friendly. Still, there are some very good deals available for agents if you know where and how to look, and Jade knows.

Her personal favorite is taking cruises. They have everything she can possibly want. Good food, nice accommodations, lots of activities, getting to see a new city or country every day or two. Not to mention onboard spa facilities. She's personally addicted to massages especially the hot stone variety.

A day of pure heaven on a cruise ship starts with a light breakfast, then moves on to a morning dive on a wonderful coral reef in the Caribbean, possibly Aruba or Bon Aire. Upon returning to the ship, bring your wet suit and other equipment up to the highest of the pool decks. You shower them off to remove the salt and grit, and lay them on a lounge chair to dry.

You get a large fruity umbrella drink and soak in the hot tub while waiting for the sun to do its job. When the first drink is finished, it's usually time to turn everything over. After the second, it's time to go shower and change for lunch. After lunch, time for your Hot Stone massage, then all that's left is a nap until dinner. If things have gone properly, you aren't napping alone! An evening of shows, gambling and dancing lead to the Midnight Buffet, complete with its tower of chocolate. That is one Perfect Day!

It is still a fantasy, the diving cruise anyway, but someday she will have the time and money to have that Perfect Day at sea. As a certified Dive Travel Agent, any client that comes in looking for a vacation package and wants more than a resort- dive, the Sisters send on to Jade. While doing research for these clients she has amassed quite a list of places she hopes to visit some day. "Enough fantasy," Jade tells herself, "time to get back to business." She opens the top file on her desk and picks up the phone.

Chapter 2

Wednesday
12 Sept '07

"Surprise, Mummy!" The twins laughed as they climbed on the big four-poster bed, "We got you presents and Pappa is having Cook make a fancy breakfast even though it isn't Sunday, all because it's your birthday." Their voices were so jumbled together it was hard to tell who was saying what.

"Children, calm yourselves, please." Jeanette said while trying to gather them in a big hug. Looking towards the doorway, she saw Jackson standing there laughing.

"Well, you might help, you know?" She laughed.

"And spoil all their fun? Would I do that, Jeanee?" was his reply. He came into the room scooping up James, as Jeanette managed to grab onto Jasmine.

"You two need to let your mother finish waking up and get dressed, if you want to have that fancy breakfast." Jack said to the children, in a fake stern voice.

"Yes, Sir!" they both replied together, trying not to laugh. Jack set down James as Jeanette let go of Jasmine, and the kids ran from the room. With a wink and a smile, Jack closed the door after them and returned to the bed.

"May I help you with your nightclothes?"   He asked, untying her nightgown as he kissed her.
"But, Sir!   What will the servants think?"   Jeanette asked in a mockingly shocked voice.

"Whatever I pay them to think. Or in this case, what I pay them NOT to think!" He laughed. "Jeanee, you're so beautiful, I'm the luckiest man in England, Europe, the whole world!"

Jade awakens from this dream feeling wrapped in love. "This is two nights in a row," she thinks, "and getting Hot! I wonder what my psyche is trying to tell me," she asks herself. "Strange that they both have twins, same as I do a boy and girl. Yes, they run on my side, my mother's side, I mean, but still. They're both about birthdays, what's with that? Mine is not until November, 11/11/77 always loved to repeat that date, the way it singsongs. Today is September twelfth, so it's not for 2 months yet. Does that mean anything? Should I know? Do I care?"

Hearing the shower running, she gets out of bed, undressing on her way. "This is the nice part of waking up early and horny," she laughs to herself. "Hey stranger." she says, as she steps in the shower with Jake, "Fancy meeting you here."

"I'm getting to enjoy this shower thing you've got going lately. Can this be a regular part of the morning routine?" He asks with a smile and a kiss.

"Only if you wash behind your ears like a good little boy. Or maybe I should do that for you?"

"Wait! You did the washing yesterday, I get to do it today. After all, we are an equal opportunity family!"

"Are we now? Well then hop to it mister, I'm getting cold!" On they played.

Looking at the clock, Jade wonders if it is going to stay this slow all day, or if they will get busier after lunch. "It's only 11:00 am," she muses, "and I guess people are busy with other errands." She is looking down at her screen when she hears the door chime as a client walks in.

"How are you this fine day?" She asks the nice looking man in the Irish woolen cap.

"I'm having a great day, and it'll be even better if you can send me to the Isles." He replies.

"Would that be the British Isles, or the Caribbean you had in mind?" is her inquiry.

"Oh, the Irish actually. I'm sorry. I was thinking about them, and just thought you could read my mind." He laughs as he takes a seat at her desk.

"Not to worry, I do that all the time. Luckily, my husband and kids are quite good at guessing what I'm thinking. Now when did you plan to travel, and will you be alone? I'm Jade Worth by the way, and you are?"

"I'm Dave Geddes, my sister and myself will be traveling the last week of April and/or the first two of May. I understand that's a shoulder season and the weather's not too bad."

"Ahhh, I see you've been doing your homework. That's great, it makes my job so much easier. Yes, early May is a great time to go. The shoulder s
season is such a price savings, the way it spans the higher priced Spring Break/Easter Holiday and Summer vacation periods.

The price is right, and the weather isn't bad either. When I was in Ireland last year, we had morning drizzle and afternoon sun. As most tours do the driving in the morning, the rain isn't that big of a problem. How long did you have in mind? Where in particular did you want to go? Were you looking for a motor coach tour? Or a self-drive with the hotels pre booked? Do you have a budget in mind?" Jade takes out her pad and begins to take notes.
"Ok, let's see if I can remember them in order. We are thinking 10-14 days. We want the self-drive with hotels, but one with some

flexibility, so we can wander if we want to. Day tours in some cities, and left to ourselves a lot. Both Irelands, I want to see the Giant's Causeway and Belfast, as well as Dublin and Killarney, and that's just for starters.

For a budget, we really aren't sure. We have $10,000 saved, but would prefer not to spend all of it on the travel part. We need some for food, and the fun stuff we'll find. I'm sure we'll manage to find a shop or two to enjoy." Dave wraps up.

"Well, with that kind of time and money, you might also include Scotland if you have any interest. It could be a two-for-one sale." Jade answers.
"We might think about that. We were expecting to have to save up and visit Scotland next year. If its doable in one trip that could be great."

"Let me get a few of the brochures I think would work for you, while you fill out this customer info sheet for me." Jade says, handing him the sheet and a pen. She walks back to the racks of pamphlets and flyers to find the two she has in mind.

Seeing that he's done, she walks over with the information and says, "These two are the best choices for what you're looking to do. Why don't you read them over and stop back early next week to start the planning phase. Will your sister be here to discuss the itinerary?"

"No," Dave replies, "She lives south of D.C. I'm doing all the planning, and just keeping her up to date. My schedule over at St. John's College gives me more flexibility than her job does."

"That's good for you, and me too." Jade smiles, "What do you teach?"

"Native American Studies. I'm ¼ Cree and ¾ Scot/Irish. It makes for an interesting family dinner." Dave grins. "My full name is David Three Feathers Geddes. I only use that for my classes. Speaking of which, I should be going. Thanks so much for all your help." He shakes Jade's hand and walks out leafing through the top brochure.

Chapter 3

Thursday
13 Sept '07

"Liebhabering? Are you awake? Johanna?" Her husband whispered in her ear as she was slowly becoming conscious. "I'd like to give you your first birthday gift," he said with a twinkle in his voice.

"Not that again....Jarvis, you give me the same thing every year." She replied in mock annoyance, but couldn't stifle her laughter as he started to tickle her. They'd just started to kiss when the door burst open, and two kids jumped on the bed.

"I told you she was awake." The little girl said, half-playful, half-bratty.

"But Vater said to wait until HE opened the door," replied her brother, not really whining.

"Well I guess it's too late for that now. Come on kids, let's all kiss Mutter 30 times for her 30th Geburtstag!" So saying, they all tackled Johanna and kissed her everywhere they could manage. On her face, her neck, her arms, her hands; it became a wrestling match.

"Enough! Peace! I surrender! Let me up and I'll make you all some breakfast. You two go and get dressed, and we'll be down in a bit. Jan, be my big boy and put some more coals on the fires, but don't smother them. Joselyn, please get the table ready for breakfast. Ich Liber Dich Alles!"

The twins scampered out of the room, closing the door as they went. Johanna turned back to her Jarvis. "Now, what about that present? I think you were about to unwrap it?"

"I think I can manage to find something to amuse you, Schatzi, I know you like kisses here..." He said, trailing kisses up her arm towards her throat. "And here..." Now behind her ear, and nibbling on her lobe... "And here..." covering her mouth in a passionate kiss.

"This is getting ridiculous," thinks Jade as she wakes this third morning. "I feel like I'm watching some erotic movies. I have to find a way to stop these dreams. Then again, the side bennies are fun and Jake's still in the shower. Wonder if he's waiting for me?" She undresses, and tiptoes in, finding Jake smiling as he washed so slowly he was obviously waiting for her. It was even more obvious the lower you looked.

Later, as they are finishing dressing Jade comments playfully, "I've never started my morning's feeling quite so clean before."

Jake actually blushes, which has Jade laughing out loud. After almost twelve years of marriage, and 9-year-old twins, it isn't easy to make her husband blush! "Score points for me!" she says, making a motion with her index finger in the air. This has him blushing harder. In sympathy, she walks over and gives him a hug and a big, sloppy kiss. She returns to the bathroom counter to finish getting ready, laughing all the way.

As they are leaving the house that morning Jake says in mock sternness, "We do have to either start getting up earlier, or take faster showers. I can't be late for my first hour class again. It isn't very Lieutenant Commander-ish."

"Aye-aye, Lieutenant," laughs Jade, throwing a badly executed salute. "I can't help it if you're so cute when you're wet." They move to their cars after one long goodbye kiss.

Jade loves working in Annapolis, with its quaint streets, serious history, and wonderful shops. Working there is great, and makes lunchtime fun with the great variety of cafes, bistros, or restaurants. There is plenty of day-to-day shopping around town as well, but for serious shopping she goes to Annapolis Mall.

The family lives in an older neighborhood, north of the Naval Academy, still in an Annapolis zip code, but just barely. Their split-level house isn't the largest in the area, but the lot is. They have almost 3 acres, with three sides of the home ringed by trees.
The house is set back farther than most from the street, making it look very picturesque, especially in the winter with a blanket of snow. The rear yard holds a variety of gardens, from flower to vegetable to herbal, and one for the twins that couldn't really be classified as they tended to plant whatever they find. Some of which isn't actually composed of plant matter.

There are four spacious bedrooms on the upper floor of the house, with the master suite taking the full front width of that floor. The children each have their own rooms, of course, and share the hall bathroom.

The fourth room is Jade's sanctuary. She has her sewing area, her computer, her favorite overstuffed chair, and her books. There are three wall to ceiling bookcases, crammed full of books. Additional shelves are over the computer and the sewing machine, and also overloaded. Still more books are on the table near the chair and on the floor. She really loves to lose herself in a good book.

One bookcase is for the "Special" books, the collections and single titles that are signed by the authors, they are the forever keepers. Others are just favorites she reads every few years. There is a sack that's waiting to go to the used bookstore, with a big box beside it also stuffed full of items to be resold. The room looks like chaos to most people, yet Jade can tell you where any book is at any time, and if she has a particular book or not.

She'd started studying Library Science in college, until she found that the more she learned about the systems they were teaching her, the less she enjoyed reading. It just didn't make sense to her to work at a job that made her dislike her greatest joy.

She had changed her major to Liberal arts when Jade met Jake during the second half of her sophomore year. He was finishing his senior year of a Military History degree, and had already been accepted into the Navy's Officer Corps.

Theirs was a whirlwind romance. She dropped out of college that summer and started working to save for their future. Once he was through with his Naval Officer Training and got his first assignment at Norfolk Naval Station, they were married.

What a life so far: three and three-quarters of a year at Norfolk, four years in Jacksonville Naval Air Station, and three and a half at the Academy. It has been an interesting career. With Jake up for promotion to Lieutenant Commander this summer, they will be moving again.

This is the first house they've owned, and they will have to decide if they should sell it or rent it. A lot will depend on where they are assigned next. What the housing is like at the new base, and if it is even available. What the schools are like that are associated with the housing, the kids education is very important. Will Jade be able to find a job? Will they be in an area that will even make her working worthwhile? So much to consider.

Today is her half-day at Three Sisters. Jade works most Sundays 12-4 PM; this way she has a half-day during the week to run errands. She is also off most Saturdays for family day. That is very important to her, as a parent. She mentally writes out a list of errands to run during her afternoon as she drives into work, hoping she'll have time to get them all done.

Chapter 4

Tuesday
18 Sept '07

She awoke slowly to the sounds of the little ones sleeping, knowing the sun was just beginning its rise. The arm around her slowly tightened as Black Hawk whispered, "Morning, my little Wolf, what do you wish on your birthing day?"

Smiling, Lilac Wolf turned to face her lover, her soul mate, her reason for being, and gently kissed him. "This is all I want. To be like this forever."

"That would spoil the kits' surprises, but if you wish…" and laughing, he rolled to her and started her morning with the softest kiss. Slowly it grew stronger, as his hands lightly caressed her ear lobes and teased her neck. Trailing kisses across her chin, he began nibbling on a sensitive lobe, and licking that lovely spot right behind it.

Lilac Wolf stretched her body so it was lined up better with his, and gave a bit of a purr. Slowly she ran her hand in circles on her Hawk's outer thigh. Softly enough to tickle… not that a great warrior could be tickled of course! As he started kissing down her throat, she started caressing up his thigh.

Hawk was kissing lower and lower, she was circling higher and higher. Both were trying to keep their moans of pleasure quiet, so the kits stayed asleep. Just as she reached that sensitive crease between leg and body, he took her nipple in his mouth. She gasped with pleasure, her whole body on fire.

They had barely finished when both kits were on top of them "The sun rises, your day is here!" The little ones exclaimed. "Are you going to stay in the furs forever? We can see the light."

"Now Turq, you know I get this one day to enjoy the furs until the sun is over the rivers edge. Would you have me spoil the surprise of your aunts, as they make my birth morning meal?"

"It's not our sire's day, why does he stay in the furs?" asked Grey pup.

"It's my job to keep her warm," answered Black Hawk, with a smile for the boy, and a wink for Lilac Wolf." It wouldn't do for her to catch a chill on this day would it?" he asked, trying to look serious.

"I guess not," said the pup, with his head hung down, "I wouldn't like that."

"I wouldn't either," piped up Turquoise chick.

"Why so glum little pup?" asked Lilac Wolf.

"I can't give you your birth gift in the hut. Now I have to wait for the sun, and it moves so slowly," he pouted.

Black Hawk stepped into his leggings and moccasins, picked up Grey pup and carried him out of the hut.

"And you? You're being rather quiet my little chick."

"I can wait; my gift can be given any time." Turq said with a smile. She helped her mother dress in her best buckskin tunic and leggings; braid feathers into her hair; put on her necklaces of shells and beads; slip on her moccasins; and drape a raccoon skin cape over her shoulder. Then they shook out the furs, and stacked them away, setting the hut in order for the day.

Waking, Jade realizes it's been exactly one week since she'd had the first dream about Lilac Wolf. This one started out the same, but continued on, as if the movie was playing the next part. She feels like she's there this time, like she is watching it in person.

"This is just crazy", she says aloud, as she rises from the bed.

"Did you say something?" asks Jake, from the bathroom. Looking in as he dries his hair with a towel.

"No, I'm just talking to myself, had another of those dreams."

"Damn, I knew I should have taken a longer shower." Jake says with a leer. Then he notices the look of concern on Jade's face. "What's wrong hun? Did something else happen?"

"Kind of, it was the Indians again, I mean, Native Americans. Only this time it didn't stop with the kissing. It continued on to some interesting petting, and then just switched to their kids, and getting dressed stuff.

I was there this time though. It wasn't just watching a movie; I was in it, or watching it from the inside. That's what I was thinking when I woke up. It's kind of left me feeling unsettled."

"I can see that." Jake says as he wraps his arms around her. "Anything I can do?"

"This is just perfect, give me a few more moments of this and I'll be good to go."

"Any time, sweets, you know that, I'm always here for you."

"Yeah, I know. That's what makes everything so perfect in my life. But, I hear Jen and Jer in the kitchen, we'd better hurry if we don't want to have to remodel," she chuckles.

Looking out the window at the City Docks while sitting at her desk is one of the reasons Jade enjoys working at the Three Sisters. The other one is the Sisters themselves. There are actually only two of them, Alice and Alicia. They named the Agency after their favorite set of books by Nora Roberts, "the Three Sisters Trilogy". She just loved that about the women.

Both sisters are widows; their husbands were killed in the same drunk driving accident, as they were going to the store on Thanksgiving Day. After taking thirty days to mourn, the women decided to move into Alice's house. They sold Alicia's home, and opened the Three Sister's Travel Agency. The sisters were left financially well off, with neither needing to work, yet they thought it would be fun to share all their travel knowledge with others. Not to mention keeping them busy so they wouldn't get too crazy as young widows, they were only 50 and 52. Yep, you just had to love women who thought like that.

Jade notices Dave Geddes walking towards the Three Sisters with the brochures she gave him in his hand. He looks up and waves upon seeing her smile at him. She meets him at the door and motions towards her desk.
"How has the homework been going?" She asks.

"Just great! We've gotten a good idea of what we want. Now I just need you to tell me if it's at all doable." He answers with a laugh.

"That's what I'm here for." Is her cheery reply, and they settle down to work.

Handing Jade the brochures, opened to specific pages David says, "We've decided to just stay in Ireland and really explore the country this year. We'll visit Scotland next year. We like this self drive package, and then some of the city tours in this other one, can we do that?"

"Certainly, that's easy," answers Jade. "I was afraid you wanted something hard. The city tours are meant to be 'ala cart' so you can book them for just the cities you want. In addition, they're on a voucher system, just like the hotels in your self-drive, so you won't be locked into set dates. When you arrive, you call the number and set up your tour. If you know you'll be there in advance, you can pre-book them.

Just be sure you'll be there, if you miss a time for a scheduled tour, you will lose it. They won't wait past the listed pick-up times, and they won't refund you a cent, unless you call 24 hours ahead. That's why I always recommend waiting until you have arrived. You just never know what may happen, especially on the roads in Ireland.

Let me get your paperwork together. I'll make your bookings after you leave. It's a lot of computer work that I doubt you want to sit through. When I have the confirmations, I'll email them to you. Your deposit of 25% will be due at that time. Your final balance is due 45 days prior to your departure. If it's easier on your budget, you may come in and make monthly payments. Most people find it's easier to manage that way, doesn't seem to hurt as much as putting down that big lump sum.

I'll be checking both commercial and discount air, booking this far in advance, we should find some good prices. If the best rate I can find is a scheduled non-refundable ticket, the full amount will be due when it's booked. However, we can discuss the pros and cons of that if it happens. Otherwise, I'll need a 25% deposit when it's confirmed and the balance on the air is due 60 days out. Do you have any other questions?" Jade asks with a smile. She knows sometimes she talks too fast and forgets to come up for air.

"When should we get our passports?" asks David.

"I would get them now. Starting January first next year, everyone needs them. All the people who have traveled for years without them will suddenly find out that they need them now. It's going to be crazy, so don't wait. This way if something happens, or the application gets lost, you have plenty of time to apply again. The three to six months of availability you save on the other end just isn't worth the peace of mind now."

"Great. Then that's what we'll do. I'm planning on calling Mary tonight anyway, so I'll let her know not to wait."

"Well, I think that just about wraps everything up nice and neatly," says Jade. "But I have a professional question for you."
"Sure, what can I do for you?" asks Dave.

"This is going to sound odd...um...I've been having this strange dream, about this Native American woman, on her 30th birthday. I was wondering if there was any way to find out if this tribe ever existed. Or if my imagination just made it up from all the things I've read and seen on T.V."

"I guess you could tell me about her and anything else you see. I could check it out and see if I can find a tribe that matches. What was her name?"

"Lilac Wolf, and her husband, or at least her mate, and the father of her kids, is called Black Hawk. The kids were Turquoise chick, and Grey pup. I got the feeling that the color names are permanent but the chick and pup indicated male and female...and were baby names. They would have adult names in the future. How could I know that?" Jade asks, slightly confused.

"Many tribes give the children baby names, or name them for their parents until they are of age to be considered an adult in the tribe. Usually the boy's first hunting kill, and the girl's first period were considered the ages of adulthood-around 10 or 12 summers, depending on when they were born, and the tribe they were in.

Why don't you write down everything you remember, and email me the list? Here's my card, I'll put my home email on the back. I check it through out the day. So whenever you get the chance, just send it to me, and I'll see what I can find out."

"Thanks Dave, I know this sounds silly, but these dreams feel real, like I know her somehow. So...I guess I should at least try to find out what tribe she belonged to. Maybe I'm just going crazy," she laughs. "Thanks for the help."

"Considering what I'm about to put you through with this trip, it's the least I can do. I'll get back to you as soon as I can find anything. I'll talk to you soon. And you let me know when you need those deposits, ok?"

"Don't worry, that's not something I'm likely to forget. Enjoy the rest of this nice weather. And I'll talk to you soon." Jade says as she walks Dave to the door, and waves him out.

Turning back towards her desk, she wonders if she's just made a big fool of herself in front of her client. It doesn't feel that way. Dave is a very nice, friendly person. She just hopes he doesn't think she's too unstable.

Chapter 5

Wednesday
19 Sept '07

"Surprise, Mummy!" The twins laughed as they climbed on the big four-poster bed, "We got you presents and Pappa is having Cook make a fancy breakfast even though it isn't Sunday, all because it's your birthday." Their voices were so jumbled together it was hard to tell who was saying what.

"Children, calm yourselves, please." Jeanette said while trying to gather them in a big hug. Looking towards the doorway, she saw Jackson standing there laughing.

"Well, you might help, you know?" She laughed.

"And spoil all their fun? Would I do that, Jeanee?" was his reply. He came into the room scooping up James, as Jeanette managed to grab onto Jasmine.

"You two need to let your mother finish waking up and get dressed, if you want to have that fancy breakfast." Jack said to the children, in a fake stern voice.

"Yes, Sir!" they both replied together, trying not to laugh. Jack set down James as Jeanette let go of Jasmine, and the kids ran from the room. With a wink and a smile, Jack closed the door after them and returned to the bed.

"May I help you with your nightclothes?" He asked, untying her nightgown as he kissed her.

"But, Sir! What will the servants think?" Jeanette asked in a mockingly shocked voice.

"Whatever I pay them to think. Or in this case, what I pay them NOT to think!" He laughed. "Jeanee, you're so beautiful, I'm the luckiest man in England, Europe, the whole world!"

Kissing, they fell back together. Slowly Jackson unbuttoned the gown that Jeanette wore, one button at a time, kissing the bared skin as he went. He usually hated these high-necked styles, but this was fun. Under the chin, on the throat, that cute little cleft where the collarbones meet, where her locket hangs, at the top of her cleavage, deep in the middle, at the bottom. This could take hours, as he leisurely drew circles along the edges of her breasts.

Jeanette let out a low moan. She had been trying to pretend indifference, being still, with a haughty look on her face. But a woman could only resist so much. Every nerve she had was tingling. She knew it wasn't "lady like" but she finally took his head and moved it to one exposed breast and said softly "Please!" That's all he'd been waiting for.

Walking into the breakfast room, painted in creams and yellows to accent the easterly facing windows, Jeanette and Jackson were in full hunting regalia.

"Oh, Look! Mummy has on her new boots. I told you Pappa would give them to her before they came down," came Jasmine's very grown up comment.

"I thought so too," said James, "I'm just not bragging about it. Look at all your presents Mummy. These two are from me!"

"Everything looks wonderful, and those two look perfect James. I bet you wrapped them yourself as well." She laughed.

"How did you know?" James asked, looking rather confused in that little boy way.

"Just look at it, anyone can tell," sniped Jasmine.

"That wasn't very nice." Jackson snapped. "Boys his age aren't as artistic as girls are."

"Yeah! But I can run faster than you, and I can fish better too…so there!" James said.

Just as things were about to get heated between the kids, Dolly, the cook, came in carrying a big platter of eggs and sausages. Sally, the scullery maid, followed carrying bacon, and biscuits, and puddings, and pastries; all the makings of a fancy breakfast. Nancy, the downstairs maid, came over to pour the tea, and serve the meal. She'd been with the family for 5 years now and knew exactly what every one wanted.

Conversation during the meal centered on the Birthday hunt: Who would be here, who couldn't make it and why. Which children were likely to attend, and how far they would be allowed to ride with the hunt. Who would be Nanny this year? Would Uncle Milton's horse throw him again? This was always a great topic for discussion.

Jade can't believe it. She wakes up feeling confused, annoyed and betrayed by her own mind. "Now it's the English Lady, Jeanette!" She thinks, "and I'm in her movie. What the hell is going on here? I have to stop this. Yes, the sex is getting better…but that's not the point. And why is Jake already gone this morning? Did he really have to go to that staff meeting? Ok, so maybe he did, but I want him Now!"

"Great Jade," she says aloud, "you're sounding like James!" Disgusted at the thought, she gets up and walks into the bathroom. Guess I have to shower alone today. At least I get all the hot water!" Finally smiling, she turns the water to boiling, and enters.

As she arrives in the kitchen, she finds a disaster. 'Not-Me' has spilled milk and cereal everywhere. She knows when she asks who the culprit is the answer from both her kids will be 'Not-Me'. Being twins, they stand up for each other by never being guilty of anything. It's always this poor poltergeist, Not-Me or his friends I-don't-know, and I-forget.

"Would one of you at least care to explain this mess as you clean it up?" she asks the twins, who are sitting at the counter, eating their cereal like little angles.

"They just flew out of our hands; it isn't our fault, honest Mom." They both answer in unison.

"And we know you will be mad if we don't finish eating before school, so we finished eating first and now we can clean it up," piped up Jenyfer hopping off her stool. She is the older of the two, by only 4 minutes and 36 seconds, which she never lets Jeremy forget, and their natural leader.

Looking at the clock, Jade realizes the bus will be here any minute, so once again, the kids are saved. She gathers up their book bags and hustles them off to the corner. "I'll just have to clean it up myself," she thinks. "I'd only have to redo it anyway;" she chuckles as she goes to get the small wet-vac.

Walking back into the room, she can't help noticing that the milk is only on the washable parts of the wall. Some how it has missed the wallpaper, and the decorative plants she has hanging overhead, just the floor and the baseboards and the doorframe are wet. "Very interesting, some days I wish I could be a fly on the wall to find out what those two are up to. Then again, I guess I'm probably better off not knowing."

Once the room is no longer crunchy or sticky, she sets out for her office. Both Alice and Alicia love to hear about the twin's latest adventures, and Jade has such a talent for telling the stories. Jade always loved reading and story telling. One of her fondest memories is reading with her great-grandmother as a small child. Her brother and sister always got bored after a few pages, but Jade could sit for hours and read aloud.

Jade always read to the twins, even while she was pregnant. Now that they are reading so well the nightly routine has the twins curling up on one of their beds and each reading a chapter from the latest book.

The current book is the Swiss Family Robinson. Jeremy wants to live on an island, and Jeny insists that she would never set foot any place that did not have running water and indoor toilets. Jen's idea of roughing it was a no-name motel, while Jer is in Cub Scouts with his dad and would go camping every weekend if he could.

Jade is a bit of a writer herself, mostly bits of poetry here and there, short stories that pop into her head now and then. She writes a few pieces for the quarterly newsletter at work. Some day she'll sit down and just write, maybe when the twins are in college. However, that's too far away to think about now, she's arrived at work.

Chapter 6

Thursday
20 Sept '07

*"Liebhabering? Are you awake? Johanna?" Her husband whispered
in her ear as she was slowly becoming conscious. "I'd like to give you
your first birthday gift," he said with a twinkle in his voice.*

*"Not that again...Jarvis, you give me the same thing every year." She
replied in mock annoyance, but couldn't stifle her laughter as he started
to tickle her. Turning her gently, they'd just started to kiss when the
door burst open, and two kids jumped on the bed.*

"I told you she was awake." The little girl said, half-playful, half-bratty.

*"But Vater said to wait until HE opened the door," replied her brother,
not really whining.*

*"Well I guess it's too late for that now. Come on kids, let's all kiss
Mutter 30 times for her 30th Geburtstag!" So saying, they all tackled
Johanna and kissed her everywhere they could manage. On her face,
her neck, her arms, her hands; it became a wrestling match.*

*"Enough! Peace! I surrender! Let me up and I'll make you all some
breakfast. You two go and get dressed, and we'll be down in a bit. Jan,
be my big boy and put some more coals on the fires, but don't smother
them. Joselyn, please get the table ready for breakfast. Ich Liber Dich
Alles!"*

The twins scampered out of the room, closing the door as they went. Johanna turned back to her Jarvis. "Now about that present? I think you were about to unwrap it?"

"I think I can manage to find something to amuse you Schatzi, I know you like kisses here..." He said, trailing kisses up her arm towards her throat. "And here..." Now kissing behind her ears, and nibbling on her ear lobe. "And here..." covering her mouth in passion.

Jarvis was quite a kisser, each one even deeper than the last; it was like he was trying to climb inside her heart, as it was melting into his. Both sets of hands were removing clothes, and caressing warm skin. Petting and playing, while the kisses continued to evolve into a total union of breaths and souls.

"Wow! This is getting steamy. Speaking of steamy, do I hear the shower? Why I think I do, I guess I'll just go work off some of this pent up energy." Jade continues talking to herself as she walks into the shower and joins Jake. It takes quite a while for all that energy to properly dissipate.

"I have to say, my thighs are getting stronger from all this 'showering' we've been doing lately" Jade teases Jake as he shaves and she applies her makeup.

"Ouch! Don't make me laugh when I'm shaving," he chuckles. "This has three very sharp blades in it. So I get three cuts for the price of one."

"Aww here let me kiss it all better for you." Jade coos. "That will make the boo-boo go bye-bye for the little baby."
"OK, that's enough of that. I'm a big studly man; I'll have you know. I think I've been proving that rather well lately! I just don't like getting all cut up shaving. Is that so wrong?"

"I guess I can cut you some slack this time," she laughs, as she finishes her face. "Anything else you need cut while I'm at it?"

"No I think I'm good. We'll just save the cutting for paper if it's all right with you." Jake teases back. "And I do know what you mean about the thighs and glutes. I've been feeling rather trim my self these days! Keep up the good work, and we'll both be hotter that ever by summer"

"I hope like hell these dreams are over by summer, but that doesn't mean the morning showers have to be. It's put a lot of spring into my step lately, even the Sisters have noticed, and you know how oblivious they can tend to be.

Well let's get moving mister, daylight's burning!" Jade gave Jake a kiss and a swat on the buns and went to get dressed.

Chapter 7

Tuesday
25 Sept '07

She awoke slowly to the sounds of the little ones sleeping, knowing the sun was just beginning its rise. The arm around her slowly tightened as Black Hawk whispered, "Morning, my little Wolf, what do you wish on your birthing day?"

Smiling, Lilac Wolf turned to face her lover, her soul mate, her reason for being, and gently kissed him. "This is all I want. To be like this forever."

"That would spoil the kits' surprises, but if you wish..." and laughing, he rolled to her and started her morning with the softest kiss. Slowly it grew stronger, as his hands lightly caressed her ears lobes and teased her neck. Trailing kisses across her chin, he began nibbling on the sensitive lobe, and licking that lovely spot right behind it.

Lilac Wolf stretched her body so it was better lined up with his, and gave a bit of a purr. Slowly she ran her hand in circles on her Hawk's outer thigh. Softly enough to tickle... not that a great warrior could be tickled of course! As he started kissing down her throat, she started caressing up his thigh.

Hawk was kissing lower and lower, she was circling higher and higher. Both were trying to keep their moans of pleasure quiet, so the kits stayed asleep. Just as she reached that sensitive crease between leg and body,

39

he took her nipple in his mouth. She gasped with pleasure, her whole body on fire.

They had barely finished when both kits were on top of them "The sun rises, your day is here!" The little ones exclaimed. "Are you going to stay in the furs for ever? We can see the light."

"Now Turq, you know I get this one day, to enjoy the furs until the sun is over the river's edge. Would you have me spoil the surprise of your aunts, as they make me my birth morning meal?"

"It's not our sire's day, why does he stay in the furs?" asked Grey pup.

"It's my job to keep her warm," answered Black Hawk, with a smile for the boy, and a wink for Lilac Wolf. "It wouldn't do for her to catch a chill on this day would it?" he asked, trying to look serious.

"I guess not," said the pup, with his head hung down, "I wouldn't like that."

"I wouldn't either," piped up Turquoise chick.

"Why so glum little pup?" asked Lilac Wolf.

"I can't give you your birth gift in the tepee. Now I have to wait for the sun, and it moves so slowly," he pouted.

Black Hawk stepped into his leggings and moccasins, picked up Grey pup and carried him out of the hut.

"And you? You're being rather quiet my little chick."

"I can wait; my gift can be given any time." Turq said with a smile. She helped her mother dress in her best buckskin tunic and leggings; braid feathers into her hair; put on her necklaces of shells and beads; slip on her moccasins; and drape a raccoon skin cape over her shoulders. Then they shook out the furs and stacked them away, setting the hut in order for the day.

Mother and daughter left the hut and walked towards the central fire, hand in hand. Others were gathering, everyone called greetings to Lilac

Wolf and Turquoise chick. It was a happy, loving, family feeling that enveloped the scene in an early morning mist. The fire was blazing with many cook pots around it. Blankets and furs had been spread around the sunny end of the clearing. All the children were running and playing as if this was a holiday.

Thirty summers, thought Lilac Wolf, where did it all go? I feel as young as Turquoise and Grey, yet I'm to be entering the elder woman's counsel this night. I start my year of trial. Am I ready? Can I really lead the women? Can I stand up to the men? I don't feel all that wise today. Will I be in only 1 year? It seems so long and yet so short. How is this possible? Why have I been so blessed?

Lilac Wolf looked around her. They were a small village of Catawba, only seven hands of huts, in rough circles on the west edge of the Iswa river. The long house was facing the water and the morning sun with the ceremonial fire in the clearing before it. The sweat lodge was to the north, and the woman's lodge way off to the south, all surrounded by young tree trunks dug into the earth to form a barrier. One opening was easier to defend, from their enemies and from the bears that liked to raid their camp. Small fields now lay fallow, just past the edge of the village; the sun was shining on the water, as it slowly passed the horizon.

She said a silent prayer of thanks to "He who Never Dies", then joined her family for the celebration. She was led to a place of honor and seated on a large bearskin. Her sister brought her a bowl of apples and nuts to start the meal. An aunt served a mash of squash and corn with honey in it, and some roasted rabbit from this morning's kill. The tea like beverage of herbs was warm and spicy as Turquoise chick handed her a small cup.

Confused, Jade looks around, expecting to see the fire. She still feels its warmth, smells its smoke. She has the taste of the beverage on her tongue, the sounds of the people talking in her ears. This time she was Lilac Wolf's shadow, almost her, but not quite. She understood what everyone was saying, who they all were. She knew which hut they lived in, and with whom.

"It's Tuesday. That makes this the third Tuesday in a row. Am I going to have this dream every Tuesday from now on? That's a scary thought. I'd better write down everything I can remember for David. I'm sure he's going to be interested. He'll be in to make his deposit this week. The Iswa River? Never heard of it. Guess that's what Map-Quest is for. The same goes for Catawba. Wonder if there is a place named that, or a river for that matter. Iswa and Catawba seem to be interchangeable. Hmmm. Hope David's up to this." Jade muses.

"Well you aren't gonna find it here." She laughs aloud! She threw back her covers and heads for the shower, dropping her gown on the way. Jake would pick today to go in early. "Wait until I tell him all about this stuff." She giggles, as she steps into the stall, turning on the water.

"Hi, David," Jade says, looking up to find her client standing at her desk. She's been so intent on her work she hasn't even heard him come in.

"Hi, I had some time so I thought I'd drop off the money. Is this a good time?" he asks.

"It's always a good time to get money," she smiles, "just let me put this aside, and get out your file." Jade neatens her desk and pulls the proper file from her drawer. "Let's see here, you owe me two million dollars right?" She asks.

David does a double take, and then laughs. "You had me for a minute there."

"Yeah, I know, but now anything I say will seem so little! It's all in the presentation. Are you both sure about the dates? Going mid-week saves so much money, but not everyone can manage to have two weeks interrupted that way."

"Actually, it works better for both of us. It'll be like taking only one full week off this way. I know it's cheaper, and it should be less crowded too, right?"

"Normally it will be. Coming back, I'm not so sure, Ireland's University's will be out and there might be a lot of college kids traveling. You'll be surprised how many take summer jobs at resorts here or in the Caribbean. The dates vary, just like here, so it's anyone's guess. Will that be on a Visa or Master Card?"

"We're using my Visa for this payment, and my sister wants to make a payment on her Master Card next month. Can she do that?"

"Sure, just have her call me when she's ready, and I'll fax her the form. Once she fills it out, signs and dates it, all she has to do is fax it back. If she wants to continue to make payments on that same card, she can write that on the bottom, and re-sign and date below the note. She can either state the amounts and dates of the payments in her note, or fax me an authorization each time. That doesn't have to be anything too formal. Just a memo saying 'I authorize Three Sisters Agency to charge my Master Card on file for XX amount of money on XX date applied to account # DG/5 May 08.'"

"Great, well here's my plastic, let's make this official." Dave hands Jade the credit card, and she walks to the office to run it through the card machine.

Returning to her desk, Jade gives Dave the paperwork to sign, including the credit card receipt. While he's looking over everything, she says. "I had another one of those dreams about Lilac Wolf last night. They seem to happen on Monday nights or Tuesday mornings."

"Did you learn anything more about who she is, or who her tribe is?" asks Dave, looking very interested.

"They are the Catawba; the river they are on is called the Iswa, or the Catawba. I think that means 'river.' Does that make any sense to you? 'Cause it sure doesn't to me."

"Yeah, it makes a lot of sense. A natural structure or a body of water named many of the early tribes. To them the river was their life, so they were of the river. Catawba...can't say I've ever heard of them. Iswa means river, or Catawba River. I'll check into this for you. Might take me a while, we're starting a very intensive lesson this week in my freshman classes. It's their first research project, and their topics have to be approved, as well as their research materials. My free time gets eaten up pretty quickly. I'll let you know if I find out anything."

"No hurry, I just thought you might be familiar with them. I don't want you to go to a lot of trouble about this. They're just silly dreams."

"You are having them for a reason. Remember, I come from people that believe in omens and signs and spirits coming back to talk to the living. It's not a problem; it's actually very fascinating. I wish I had more time to give to it. But I should know something soon." Dave gets up from the desk, gathers his copy of the paperwork and says, "Thanks for all your help with the trip. I'll let Mary know about the faxes."

As she watches Dave leave, Jade isn't sure if she wants him to find anything or not.

Chapter 8

**Wednesday
26 Sept '07**

"Surprise, Mummy!" The twins laughed as they climbed on the big four-poster bed, "We got you presents and Pappa is having Cook make a fancy breakfast even though it isn't Sunday, all because it's your birthday." Their voices were so jumbled together it was hard to tell who was saying what.

"Children, calm yourselves, please." Jeanette said while trying to gather them in a big hug. Looking towards the doorway, she saw Jackson standing there laughing.

"Well, you might help, you know?" She laughed.

"And spoil all their fun? Would I do that, Jeanee?" was his reply. He came into the room scooping up James, as Jeanette managed to grab onto Jasmine.

"You two need to let your mother finish waking up and get dressed, if you want to have that fancy breakfast." Jack said to the children, in a fake stern voice.

"Yes, Sir!" they both replied together, trying not to laugh. Jack set down James as Jeanette let go of Jasmine, and the kids ran from the room. With a wink and a smile, Jack closed the door after them and returned to the bed.

"May I help you with your nightclothes?" He asked, untying her nightgown as he kissed her.

"But, Sir! What will the servants think?" Jeanette asked in a mockingly shocked voice.

"Whatever I pay them to think. Or in this case, what I pay them NOT to think!" He laughed. "Jeanee, you're so beautiful, I'm the luckiest man in England, Europe, the whole world!"

Kissing, they fell back together. Slowly Jackson unbuttoned the gown that Jeanette wore, one button at a time, kissing the bared skin as he went. He usually hated these high-necked styles, but this was fun. Under the chin...on the throat...that cute little cleft where the collarbones meet...where her locket hangs...at the top of her cleavage...deep in the middle...at the bottom. This could take hours, as he leisurely drew circles along the edges of her breasts.

Jeanette let out a low moan. She had been trying to pretend indifference, being still, with a haughty look on her face. A woman could only resist so much. Every nerve she had was tingling. She knew it wasn't "lady like" but she finally took his head and moved it to one exposed breast and said softly "Please!"

That's all he'd been waiting for; he lifted Jeanette up enough to remove her gown the rest of the way. "I want to see all of you," he murmured, caressing her body. "You keep getting more beautiful, even more beautiful than when we first met. More beautiful than you were last year." He started kissing all those places he had been caressing, starting back at her breasts, slowly circling to her navel, and then softly moving lower, barely touching her skin....

Walking into the breakfast room, painted in creams and yellows to accent the easterly facing windows, Jeanette and Jackson were in full hunting regalia.

"Oh, Look! Mummy has on her new boots. I told you Pappa would give them to her before they came down," came Jasmine's very grown-up comment.

"I thought so too," said James, "I'm just not bragging about it. Look at all your presents Mummy. These two are from me!"

"Everything looks wonderful, and those two look perfect James. I bet you wrapped them yourself as well." She laughed as she saw the slightly mangled cloth on the larger one, it's odd shape making it difficult for an adult to wrap properly, and impossible for a 10 year old to manage. The smaller package was much neater, if you ignored the ink smudge and the knots in the ribbon.

"How did you know?" James asked, looking rather confused in that little boy way.

"Just look at it, anyone can tell," sniped Jasmine.

"That wasn't very nice." Jackson said. "Boys his age aren't as artistic as girls are."

"Yeah! But I can run faster than you, and I can fish better too...so there!" James snapped.

Just as things were about to get heated between the kids, Dolly, the cook, came in carrying a big platter of eggs and sausages. Sally, the scullery maid, followed carrying bacon, and biscuits, and puddings, and pastries; all the makings of a Fancy breakfast. Nancy came over to pour the tea, and serve the meal. Having been with the family for over 5 years now she knew exactly what every one wanted. She was the best downstairs maid they'd ever had.

Conversation during the meal centered on the Birthday hunt: Who would be here, who couldn't make it and why. Which children were likely to attend, and how far they would be allowed to ride with the Hunt. Who would be Nanny this year? If Uncle Milton would be thrown by his horse this year? Always a great topic for discussion.

After the dishes had been cleared and the tea had been refreshed, the children each picked up their presents and stood in front of their mother.

"Oh my, well who should go first?" Jeanette asked.

"I should, me! Me!" said James, jumping up and down. "I'm oldest!"

"BY only 5 minutes," replied Jasmine, "and you went first last year."

"Did Not!" whined James

"Yes you did, with that blue scarf you gave her. I remember," was Jasmine's answer.

"Oh, yeah...then I guess it's your turn. Well hurry up. You're taking too long."

"Here mum, I made this all by myself. It's why I've been in my room reading so much lately."

"Why thank you Jasmine. What pretty paper, where did you find it?" Inquired Jeanette, smiling.

"Pappa took us into town with him last week when you went to see Aunt Susan. It was all a big surprise." Jasmine giggled. "Open it!"

Carefully, Jeanette opened the package and found a knitted bed jacket all done in light blues and greens, with a purple ribbon tie. "My! This is beautiful. Where did you learn to knit something this light and dainty? Not from me, that's for sure."

"It's actually crochet, and Sally taught me. It's really quite simple, once you have the right needle and the right thin yarns. That was the hard part. Trying to explain to Pappa what I needed when he went to town last month. But he did quite well," she said in a very adult tone.

"Yes I can see that, and so did you! I'm very proud of you. This is so very soft. I can't wait to wear it tomorrow morning. Come here so I can give you a big hug." Jeanette moved her chair away from the table so she could embrace her daughter.

"My turn now!" James said, as he pushed his presents between his mother and sister. "I made you something you really need. Not some silly old bed jacket. It's only a cape anyway."

"It's not silly; I worked very hard on that. Mum needs it to keep her shoulders warm in the mornings when she has her tea upstairs. Mummy, tell him it's not silly!" whined Jasmine.

"James, it's a very lovely bed jacket. The cape style lets me wear it over any of my gowns. Don't be bratty, or you shall spend the day in your room, and not with the others on the Hunt."

"I'm sorry, and I'm sorry to you too, Jasmine...Will you open mine now, Mummy?"

"Of course, let me put this down first." Jeanette placed the bed jacket on the table, and looked at the presents in her lap.

"The big one first, then the other one, they go together."

"That's fine, let's see what we have here..." Jeanette said as she opened the larger package. "...It's a? A? Let me take it out and get a good look at it."

"It's a jewelry holder. See, it's a hand, and you put it on its base like this." James took the smooth hand shaped piece of wood from his mother, and twisted it into the flat piece he removed from the wrappings. The hand stood up on the table.

"The fingers are curved so you can put your necklaces on them, and the thumb has holes for your earrings, and this shallow place in the base is for your hair combs. It's walnut, from that branch that fell from the tree behind the stables. And I made it all myself."

"Well, isn't that inventive, who showed you how to do all that?" an amazed Jeanette inquired. She ran her hand over the wood, feeling how wonderfully smooth it was.

"Mikey, in the stables; He does a lot of wood stuff. He let me use his knives and files and everything. He showed me how to find the right piece of wood for what we was, I mean were making. How to make the base and the stand fit together, but still be able to come apart. This is for when you travel too. So you don't have to worry where everything gets to, it's all in one place. Isn't it super? Oh! Open the other one now!"

"All right James, calm yourself a bit, I'll open it now." Jeanette *carefully opened the smaller package that was wrapped in tissue paper. "Why, what a pretty Comb. Thank you James!" she exclaimed as she pulled him into a hug. "This will match the dress I'm wearing to the dance tonight. However did you know?"*

"Jasmine helped me on that one. She saw it when we all went to town. She knew I was looking for something to put on the tray. I thought this was pretty, and I had some money, 'cause my gift didn't really cost anything. I'm glad you like it."

"I really do. It's wonderful, as is the jewelry stand. I still can't believe the two of you are so grown up and so talented. Come here for another hug, both of you!"

"Shit!" is Jade's response on awakening. "Now I'm Jeanette's shadow. Is this never going to end? And those kids...talk about spoiled brats."

"Talking to yourself again, hun?" Jake pipes in from the bathroom.

"Yeah, more of the English dream. I'm Jeanette's shadow now. Or rather her echo, I sat through a big English breakfast, and drank way too many cups of tea."

"But you hate tea!"

"Tell me about it. I still have the taste of that English breakfast stuff in my mouth. I'm coming to brush. Maybe that will help." Jade playfully butts Jake aside and reaches for the tooth gel. He moves just enough for her to get to the sink, then wraps his arms around her and starts kissing the back of her neck.

"Sorry I missed the shower, but I have to get in a bit early. I've a student meeting before class. But know I'm there with you in spirit." Jake jokes.

"Cute, really cute...in spirit! Very funny. It's not nice to pick on the mentally defective you know. I could report you to the politically correct police." Jade laughs. "They'll come and arrest you in front of your class and everything."

"Then I better get out of here before I say anything else to incriminate myself. One real kiss and I'm gone."

"You think you get a kiss after that, boy, you are dreaming! You'll have to do some serious groveling before you earn back kisses." Jade jokes back.

"OK, I'm sorry, and I'll take you out to dinner tonight just the two of us. You get the babysitter, and pick the place. Keep it under $100 for the whole evening. Will that work?" He asks.

"Hell yeah! Come over here, that gets you one heck of a kiss, and more later!" Jade kisses Jake very thoroughly, and he goes off to the Naval Academy.

Jade finishes her shower, gets dressed for the day and walks downstairs to find Jen and Jer. Surprisingly, they were both in the living room, ready for school. "OK, what are you two up to?" She asks suspiciously.

"We heard Daddy mention you going out to dinner tonight, and we want Teri to baby-sit us," answers Jeny.

"Yeah, we really like her, she plays with us. She doesn't just sit there talking to her boyfriend all night like Linda does." Pipes up Jer.

"I see, I won't even ask how you heard Daddy mention that we are going out to dinner, but if you promise to behave, I'll try Teri first. If she's already busy, I have to call Linda though, ok? Are we agreed?"

"Okay," they both agree reluctantly.

"Can you call her now, before she goes to her first class? Do you have her cell phone number?" asks Jeremy in an urgent voice.

"I'll try, but she might not have it on. I will leave a message if it's off though. Now get or you'll miss your bus." Jade kisses them both on the tops of their heads as they run out the front door. She looks up Teri's number and makes the call. Teri is available, now all she has to do is decide on a restaurant, and that is the fun part.

It is a lovely fall evening; the second night of a big harvest moon, and the temperature is a balmy 56 degrees, the perfect evening for a couple's night out. Picking the restaurant has been harder than Jade expected. There are the old stand bys, but she wants somewhere new and exciting, or at least someplace they seldom visit, someplace romantic and still affordable.

She chose Paul's on the South River in Riva, she's heard of it and noticed the ads, they just haven't ventured over to that part of town for dinner before. There are so many good restaurants in and around Annapolis proper, you just don't think of traveling, for even 10 or 12 miles. However, tonight is a perfect night for a quiet drive and a romantic dinner.

The moon on the South River, as they cross the bridge, is quite a sight. Jade is wishing she had her camera when Jake says, "That would make one hell of a photo."

"I was just thinking that!" Jade replies, "It's like you read my mind. You tend to do that a lot. It is a great location."

As they arrive at the restaurant, Jake drops Jade off at the front door before looking for a parking space. Instead of going in, she just stands looking out over the water and waits for him.

When they enter the lovely establishment they walk into a symphony of hunter green and burgundy, the plants have thousands of tiny white lights making them sparkle, and the recessed pink lighting give the whole place the softest glow. Their table is by a huge wall of windows, with a romantic view of the South River.

Yes this is the right place, Jade has picked well. She will have to thank Alice for her suggestion. Alice had attended a wedding at Paul's over the summer and mentioned it when Jade was discussing where to go that afternoon. Definitely a big thanks to Alice.

The menu choices are sublime; it takes forever to narrow it down to what they want to try the most. The couple always ends up sharing whatever they eat, it's a family thing to have a bite of this or try a taste of that, so it ends up being a joint decision.

Stuffed Mushrooms and Thai Calamari for the Appetizers, that makes a good start to the meal. They shared the Soup Sampler (a bit of both the Cream of Crab and the Wild Mushroom) for the soup course. Both the Winter White and the Jack Frost Salads sound wonderful, but their meal comes with house salads, so they decide to stay with them and just try different dressings.

Now for the Main Course! Steak Diane is one of Jake's favorites, but the Cajun Curry Scallops finally get his vote. Jade spent a lot of time going between the Rack of Lamb, Scotch Salmon, and the Macadamia Nut-Crusted Duck Breast. The duck gets the final quack.

They hold off on ordering dessert. It doesn't seem possible that there would be room for anything after all this food. A bottle of the evening's Merlot and they were set.

With the individual bottles of Voss spring water served to each guest, in place of tap water, and the excellent food and service, the evening is a great success.

Jake talks like they are dating, telling Jade things from his classes he seldom has the time to, little funny incidents that catch his sense of whimsy throughout the day. The things that have him thinking, "Jade will love that", but by the time he gets home he never remembers.

Jade recounts endless client stories; it is amazing how funny people's questions can be when planning a vacation. They discuss their children, how quickly they are growing, and how mischievous they are. They go over the possible assignments for Jake this summer when he is due for his Lieutenant Commander promotion.

Mostly they just talk like two busy working parents that finally have a chance to be together without any distractions. It is wonderful. The after dinner coffees are delicious. The whole evening is better than their first date. They promise to do this more often, much more often.

After paying Teri and locking up the house, Jake joins Jade in their bed and continues the night's communication. This time they talk with their hands and tongues, among other things.

Chapter 9

Thursday
27 Sept '07

"Liebhabering? Are you awake? Johanna?" Her husband whispered in her ear as she was slowly becoming conscious. "I'd like to give you your first birthday gift," he said with a twinkle in his voice.

"Not that again...Jarvis, you give me the same thing every year." She replied in mock annoyance, but couldn't stifle her laughter as he started to tickle her. Turning her gently, they'd just started to kiss when the door burst open, and two kids jumped on the bed.

"I told you she was awake." The little girl said, half-playful, half-bratty.

"But Vater said to wait until HE opened the door," replied her brother, not really whining.

"Well I guess it's too late for that now. Come on kids, lets all kiss Mutter 30 times for her 30th Geburtstag!" So saying, they all tackled Johanna and kissed her everywhere they could manage. On her face, her neck, her arms, her hands; it became a wrestling match.

"Enough! Peace! I surrender! Let me up and I'll make you all some breakfast. You two go and get dressed, and we'll be down in a bit. Jan, be my big boy and put some more coals on the fires, but don't smother them. Joselyn, please get the table ready for breakfast. Ich Liber Dich Alles!

The twins scampered out of the room, closing the door as they went. Johanna turned back to her Jarvis. "Now about that present? I think you were about to unwrap it?"

"I think I can manage to find something to amuse you Schatzi, I know you like kisses here..." He said, trailing kisses up her arm towards her throat. "And here..." Now kissing behind her ears, and nibbling on her ear lobe. "And here..." covering her mouth in passion.

Jarvis was quite a kisser, each one even deeper than the last; it was like he was trying to climb inside her heart, as it was melting into his. Both sets of hands were removing clothes, and caressing warm skin. Petting and playing, while the kisses continued to evolve into a total union of breaths and souls.

Johanna cooked up wursts, and potato cakes. There was kaffe and milch for das kinder. Dark brot, and butter, fresh melone, and erdbeeres, in September! "Melons and strawberries, speak English! Johanna, coffee and milk, English!" she said aloud. "The children need the English!"

So do I, living in the big city of New York, she thought. I need to speak better to do my shopping. The endless supply of foods delighted her in New York. She could find almost anything, all year round. "What a great city. To be sure it had its problems, yet it is so good to us. Jarvis has a good job. The children go to a good school, right down the block. And the ease with which I can get all the shopping done, just great."

"Fruhstuck is ready," she called. "I mean breakfast!"

As she walked into the dining room, Jarvis and the children shouted, "Alles Gute Zum Geburtstag! Happy Birthday Muter!"

Right where she had planned on placing the platter of food were gaily-wrapped packages. Jarvis took the platter, "Here let me take that. You sit, and we'll serve you today," he said smiling, and placed the platter on the sideboard.

Jan pulled out her chair and Joselyn placed a ring of flowers in her hair as Johanna sat. "This is all lovely!" She said. "I wasn't expecting you to go to this much trouble."

"YOU only turn 30 once." Jarvis grinned. "You're old as me now."

"Only for 2 weeks Vater." Joselyn laughed, as Jan poured the Kaffe. "You'll be OLD again in 2 weeks"

"Thank you for that reminder kleiner madchen, I appreciate it." Jarvis picked up Joselyn and swung her around once, putting her right back in place.

"My turn!" piped up Jan.

"I wouldn't forget you kleiner hosenmatz." Jarvis grabbed Jan and swung him harder, and plopped him down in his seat. "Time to eat before everything gets cold."

"Jake...I need you!" Jade moans as she rouses from the dream. She didn't get an answer, didn't hear the shower, and only vaguely remembers him mentioning something about a pre-class meeting." Well that sucks! Here she is playing "Casper the Ghost" with the German babe, and Jake's nowhere to be found."

"If I didn't know better, I'd think there was something else going on. There just isn't any way that man has any strength left after last night!" she laughed out loud as she dragged her self out of bed and into the shower. It just isn't as much fun all alone. It's Thursday; it should be a sexy shower day! Damn! She really needed her exercise after last night's meal.

"Guess you'll just have to take a walk at lunch, old girl," she says to herself as she plays with the shampoo suds. "What is it about these suds that make you feel like that little kid in the tub again? Ok, enough of all this noise. Stop moping and get going." Sometimes Jade has to be very strict with herself, or she will stay playing in the shower for ages.

Jade locks her front door in the morning mist; it's one of those not quite raining but more than a fog days. She hears the red shoulder hawks that nest in the trees in her front yard, and looks up to see them coasting around. The large female is calling to the three smaller males, her mate and two offspring.

Jade stands there watching for a few moments, when the mother hawk swoops over her and circles tightly directly overhead. A feeling like the hawk is trying to tell her something comes over Jade as she stands there watching the magnificent bird.

She is transfixed, unable to do anything but stare as the beautiful hawk dances across the sky. When it flies out of sight, Jade finally rouses herself. She gets into her car and takes out the notebook she always carries in her brief case. Her mind is filled with a poem that seems to write itself. She can barely get it down fast enough. It's what the hawk is telling her.

My Hawks were here
this morning
to remind me

They came
to give me warnings
of straying off again

Standing in the drizzle
watching as they flew
knowing that they knew me

3 males went East
but She kept circling
always looking my way

Why do you hesitate?
Why do you doubt?
All is in you...Believe!

As She moved West
the rain quickened
and my Heart Opened!

Jade is stunned when she's done and rereads what she's written. "Where did that come from? It's exactly how I feel, but what does it mean?" she asks out loud.

"What am I hesitating about? What do I doubt? Ok, yeah I doubt the sanity of having these weird dreams...could that be it. Could this somehow be related to the dreams? No, that is impossible. Is my mind finally snapping? Or have I just had a very mystical experience? It certainly feels like one.

How would I know? I'm not some great Medicine Woman or anything. Where did that come from? Damn it, Jade, enough of this. You are already late, now get your car in gear and get moving." As she says this she starts the car and reverses down her driveway. Once on the street, Jade takes one last look at her house, then drives off to work, running this over and over in her head.

Chapter 10

**Tuesday
2 Oct '07**

She awoke slowly to the sounds of the little ones sleeping, knowing the sun was just beginning its rise. The arm around her slowly tightened as Black Hawk whispered, "Morning, my little Wolf, what do you wish on your birthing day?"

Smiling, Lilac Wolf turned to face her lover, her soul mate, her reason for being, and gently kissed him. "This is all I want. To be like this forever."

"That would spoil the kits' surprise, but if you wish..." and laughing, he rolled to her and started her morning with the softest kiss. Slowly it grew stronger, as his hands lightly caressed her ear lobes and teased her neck. Trailing kisses across her chin, he began nibbling on the sensitive lobe, and licking that lovely spot right behind it.

Lilac Wolf stretched her body so it was better lined up with his, and gave a bit of a purr. Slowly she ran her hand in circles on her Hawk's outer thigh. Softly enough to tickle... not that a great warrior could be tickled of course! As he started kissing down her throat, she started caressing up his thigh.

Hawk kissing lower and lower, her circling higher and higher. Both were trying to keep their moans of pleasure quiet, so the kits stayed asleep. Just as she reached that sensitive crease between leg and body,

he took her nipple in his mouth. She gasped with pleasure, her whole body on fire.

After a moment of pure ecstasy, her mind cleared enough to take him in her hand and run her fingers up and down the firm thickness of him. It was her turn to make him gasp. A few well-placed caresses along the top of his magnificent manhood had him more than ready to finish pleasing her. And please her he did!

They had barely finished when both kits were on top of them "The sun rises, your day is here!" The little ones exclaimed. "Are you going to stay in the furs for ever? We can see the light."

"Now Turq, you know I get this one day, to enjoy the furs until the sun is over the river's edge. Would you have me spoil the surprise of your aunts, as they make my birth morning meal?"

"It's not our sire's day, why does he stay in the furs?" asked Grey pup.

"It's my job to keep her warm," answered Black Hawk, with a smile for the boy, and a wink for Lilac Wolf. "It wouldn't do for her to catch a chill on this day would it?" he asked, trying to look serious.

"I guess not," said the pup, with his head hung down, "I wouldn't like that."

"I wouldn't either," piped up Turquoise chick.

"Why so glum little pup?" asked Lilac Wolf.

"I can't give you your birth gift in the hut. Now I have to wait for the sun, and it moves so slowly," he pouted.

Black Hawk stepped into his leggings and moccasins, picked up Grey pup and carried him out of the hut.

"And you? You're being rather quiet my little chick."

"I can wait; my gift can be given any time." Turq said with a smile. She helped her mother dress in her best buckskin tunic and leggings; braid feathers into her hair; put on her necklaces of shells and beads; slip on

her moccasins; and drape a raccoon skin cape over her shoulders. Then they shook out the furs and stacked them away, setting the hut in order for the day.

Mother and daughter left the hut and walked towards the central fire, hand in hand. Others were gathering, everyone called greetings to Lilac Wolf and Turquoise chick. It was a happy, loving, family feeling that enveloped the scene in an early morning mist. The fire was blazing with many cook pots around it. Blankets and furs had been spread around the sunny end of the clearing. All the children were running and playing as if this was a holiday.

Thirty summers, thought Lilac Wolf, where did it all go? I feel as young as Turquoise and Grey, yet I'm to be entering the elder woman's counsel this night. I start my year of trial. Am I ready? Can I really lead the women? Can I stand up to the men? I don't feel all that wise today. Will I be in only 1 year? It seems so long and yet so short. How is this possible? Why have I been so blessed?

Lilac Wolf looked around her. They were a small village of Catawba, only seven hands of huts, in rough circles on the west edge of the Iswa river. The long house facing the water and the morning sun with the ceremonial fire in the clearing before it. The sweat lodge was to the north, and the woman's lodge way off to the south. All surrounded by young tree trunks dug into the earth to form a barrier. One opening was easier to defend, from their enemies and from the bears that liked to raid their camp. Small fields now lay fallow, just past the edge of the village; the sun was shining on the water, as it slowly passed the horizon.

She said a silent prayer of thanks to "He who Never Dies", then joined her family for the celebration. She was led to a place of honor and seated on a large bearskin. Her sister brought her a bowl of apples and nuts to start the meal. An aunt served a mash of squash and corn with honey in it, and some roasted rabbit from this morning's kill. The tea-like beverage of herbs was warm and spicy as Turquoise chick handed her a small cup.

When the eating was finished, Great Eagle, her sire and the Medicine Man, stood to begin the blessings of the day. He'd barely started when the sentries shouted alarm, "The Cherokee Come!"

63

Hearing the shouts in her ears, feeling the terror in her heart, Jade realizes she has become Lilac Wolf. In this dream, she is no longer a shadow, no more Casper. She is the Native woman. She remembers everything about her, about her life, about her family. Jade is amazed. Once she comes fully awake, the terror lifts but the memory stays.

"I can't wait to tell David," she thinks, "I'm sure he'll be interested." Jade now knows Lilac Wolf is the daughter of the Wise Woman, and was to take her mother's place this night, so her mother could step down. That's why Lilac Wolf was so concerned. She had one year to prove herself, or she'd become just another woman on the council, and her mother would have to return until her younger sister came of age in three years. If her sister isn't acceptable, then her female cousins would each be tested in order of age, until one was worthy. The shame she might bring to her family weighed heavily on her. It took a great deal of strength to put this aside and enjoy the morning meal.

Yes, she has a lot to tell David; maybe she should just call him and see if they can meet for lunch. That's a good idea; she'll call him from work and see what his schedule is like in the next few days.

She tells Jake about the latest revelations, and that she is going to ask David to lunch to catch him up to date. Jake's so preoccupied; he doesn't even tease her about going out with another man. Not that he has a reason to worry.

Driving to the Three Sisters Agency, Jade is still amazed at the clarity of the dream. She remembers everything, as if it really was her. Usually the dream's faded a lot by now. That's why she'd started writing down the highlights, especially about Lilac Wolf. What if she really is real? What if they all are?

Waving to get his attention Jade smiles as David walks over and sits down. "Thanks for coming, I know this is silly, but I have so much to tell you about Lilac Wolf, and I just can't get it all written in an e-mail," she said.

"Not a prob.," he laughs. "Actually, I'm excited. I have found a bit of information too; the Catawba tribe was absorbed by the Lumbee tribe in the mid 1700's, so very little is known about them. I'm finding this fascinating. Did I mention they were located in South Carolina, along what is still called the Catawba River? There is a Catawba city as well. So now we know where they lived."

"That's great; it felt southern, warmish for the fall. Where do you want me to begin? With the dream to give it some perspective? Then you can ask me questions? Or do you have a different order in mind?"

"No, no…that sounds great. Just tell me about the new part of the dream, and I'll take it from there. I hope you don't mind if I record this. I'll never be able to remember all of it, and I can never read my notes if I try to write things down."

The waiter arrives as he finishes speaking, so they order lunch, then Jade starts to tell David about the dream. He keeps interrupting to ask for details:

How was the hut set up? *Furs and cloths around the outside walls, with pottery stacked on one side of the fire pit in the center, which was surrounded by stones. There was a string of scalps hanging from one support. Various other implements: bows, arrows, eating spoons made of wood, a cornhusk doll.*

What was it made of? *They were round, bark covered over wood, with a hole in the roof for the smoke. They used mud to patch the holes between them, and smoothed hides on the inside walls for insulation.*

What did the village look like? *It was on the left side of the river, in a semi circle, with all doorways facing east. There were a couple rows of huts. With the Medicine Man, Wise Woman, and most important elders in the very inside, closest to the water. The most protected. To the north of the village, there was a sweat lodge for the braves, and off to the south, was the woman's hut. Poles, sort* of a palisade or wall thing, that wasn't very tightly spaced, surrounded the whole village; it was used to keep out bears and raiders.

How were they dressed? *Some of the men wore breechcloths and others wore leggings. The women wore either in long skirts or leggings and most people wore tunics. All clothing was made from buckskins. The Elders and a few other women wore cape-like coverings. Lilac Wolf's cape was made from one large raccoon. These looked more ceremonial than for warmth, they only tied at the neck, and didn't reach the waist.*

What decorations did they wear? *Lilac Wolf had necklaces of shells and beads with a few small feathers. The beads were pottery like. She must have had five or six strands; they were all bunched together so it was hard to tell. Black Hawk wore strands of beads, animal teeth and claws.*

Any in their hair? *Their hair was braided, the braves wore leather bands to help hold it in place, but the squaws didn't. Lilac Hawk did have some feathers braided into her hair for this day.*

How was it braided? *The braves had their hair braided in a simple 3-strand plait, usually in one long braid. The squaws wore theirs in two plaits, in a fancier 4-strand fashion.*

What food did they eat? *They had a variety of root vegetables and corn. Lots of nuts and berries. The meat varied from fresh fish hare and venison, to dried bear.*

How was it prepared? *The dried meat is rather obvious. The fresh were roasted with herbs, over a spit, gutted, the hare skinned, but not the fish. The venison and the vegetables were stewed in large pottery crocks, with different herbs the nuts. The corn was mashed into a paste and fried into pone*

What were considered the special or ceremonial dishes? *This bear was only eaten during a major ceremony. While they managed to kill a few every year, the bears managed to kill them too. On this hunt no one had been injured, so it was considered sacred meat, and kept for sacred days.*

What about drinks? *There was water and a hot tea like beverage. They drank in handle-less cups. Each family appeared to have their own, with their own designs on them.*

Any idea what was in the beverage? *It tasted very nutty, with a touch of fruit. I'm sure there were herbs and leaves as well.*

Jade explains about Lilac Woman becoming the Wise Woman, the trial period, and how worried she was to fail her mother and shame her family. She had been learning from her mother since she had become a squaw, as Turquoise would from her once she came of age. Now that the time had come, she was very uncertain.

Their lunch meeting takes over two and one-half hours to complete, with all the details she can remember. Luckily, it's Jade's half day, and David doesn't have any afternoon classes. He isn't sure how he's going to be able to use all the information Jade's giving him [you can't write a paper based on a dream] but he knows he has a treasure trove. When they are finally talked out, they agree to keep in touch if either have any more news, they say their goodbyes and depart.

Chapter 11

Wednesday
3 Oct '07

"Surprise, Mummy!" The twins laughed as they climbed on the big four-poster bed, "We got you presents and Pappa is having Cook make a fancy breakfast even though it isn't Sunday, all because it's your birthday." Their voices were so jumbled together it was hard to tell who was saying what.

"Children, calm yourselves, please." Jeanette said while trying to gather them in a big hug. Looking towards the doorway, she saw Jackson standing there laughing.

"Well, you might help, you know?" She laughed.

"And spoil all their fun? Would I do that, Jeanee?" was his reply. He came into the room scooping up James, as Jeanette managed to grab onto Jasmine.

"You two need to let your mother finish waking up and get dressed, if you want to have that fancy breakfast." Jack said to the children, in a fake stern voice.

"Yes, Sir!" they both replied together, trying not to laugh. Jack set down James as Jeanette let go of Jasmine, and the kids ran from the room. With a wink and a smile, Jack closed the door after them and returned to the bed.

"May I help you with your nightclothes?" He asked, untying her nightgown as he kissed her.
"But, Sir! What will the servants think?" Jeanette asked in a mockingly shocked voice.

"Whatever I pay them to think. Or in this case, what I pay them NOT to think!" He laughed. "Jeanee, you're so beautiful, I'm the luckiest man in England, Europe, the whole world!"

Kissing, they fell back together. Slowly Jackson unbuttoned the gown that Jeanette wore, one button at a time, kissing the bared skin as he went. He usually hated these high-necked styles, but this was fun. Under the chin...on the throat...that cute little cleft where the collarbones meet...where her locket hangs...at the top of her cleavage...deep in the middle...at the bottom. This could take hours, as he leisurely drew circles along the edges of her breasts.

Jeanette let out a low moan. She had been trying to pretend indifference, being still, with a haughty look on her face. A woman could only resist so much. Every nerve she had was tingling. She knew it wasn't "lady like" but she finally took his head and moved it to one exposed breast and said softly "Please!"

That's all he'd been waiting for; he lifted Jeanette up enough to remove her gown the rest of the way. "I want to see all of you," he murmured, caressing her body. "You keep getting more beautiful, even more beautiful that when we first met. More beautiful than you were last year." He started kissing all those places he had been caressing, starting back at her breasts, slowly circling to her navel, and then softly moving lower, barely touching her skin....

Walking into the breakfast room, painted in creams and yellows to accent the easterly facing windows, Jeanette and Jackson were in full hunting regalia.

"Oh, look! Mummy has on her new boots. I told you Pappa would give them to her before they came down," came Jasmine's very grown-up comment.

"I thought so too," said James, "I'm just not bragging about it. Look at all your presents Mummy. These two are from me!"

"Everything looks wonderful, and those two look perfect James. I bet you wrapped them yourself as well." She laughed as she saw the slightly mangled cloth on the larger one, it's odd shape making it difficult for an adult to wrap properly, and impossible for a 10 year old to manage. The smaller package was much neater, if you ignored the ink smudge and the knots in the ribbon.

"How did you know?" James asked, looking rather confused in that little boy way.

"Just look at it, anyone can tell," sniped Jasmine.

"That wasn't very nice." Jackson said. "Boys his age aren't as artistic as girls are."

"Yeah! But I can run faster than you, and I can fish better too...so there!" James snapped.

Just as things were about to get heated between the kids, Dolly, the cook, came in carrying a big platter of eggs and sausages. Sally, the scullery maid, followed carrying bacon, and biscuits, and puddings, and pastries, all the makings of a Fancy breakfast. Nancy came over to pour the tea, and serve the meal. Having been with the family for over 5 years now she knew exactly what every one wanted. She was the best downstairs maid they'd ever had.

Conversation during the meal centered on the Birthday hunt: Who would be here, who couldn't make it and why. Which children were likely to attend, and how far they would be allowed to ride with the Hunt. Who would be Nanny this year? If Uncle Milton would be thrown by his horse this year? Always a great topic for discussion.

After the dishes had been cleared and the tea had been refreshed, the children each picked up their presents and stood in front of their mother.

"Oh my, well who should go first?" Jeanette asked.

"I should, me! Me!" said James, jumping up and down. "I'm oldest!"

"BY only 5 minutes," replied Jasmine, "and you went first last year."

"Did Not!" whined James

"Yes you did, with that blue scarf you gave her. I remember," was Jasmine's answer.

"Oh, yeah…then I guess it's your turn. Well hurry up. You're taking too long."

"Here mum, I made this all by myself. It's why I've been in my room reading so much lately."

"Why thank you Jasmine. What pretty paper, where did you find it?" Inquired Jeanette smiling.

"Pappa took us into town with him last week when you went to see Aunt Susan. It was all a big surprise." Jasmine giggled. "Open it!"

Carefully, Jeanette opened the package and found a knitted bed jacket all done in light blues and greens, with a purple ribbon tie. "My! This is beautiful. Where did you learn to knit something this light and dainty? Not from me, that's for sure."

"It's actually crochet, and Sally taught me. It's really quite simple, once you have the right needle and the right thin yarns. That was the hard part. Trying to explain to Pappa what I needed when he went to town last month. But he did quite well," she said in a very adult tone.

"Yes I can see that, and so did you! I'm very proud of you. This is so very soft. I can't wait to wear it tomorrow morning. Come here so I can give you a big hug." Jeanette moved her chair away from the table so she could embrace her daughter.
"My turn now!" James said, as he pushed his presents between his mother and sister. "I made you something you really need. Not some silly old bed jacket. It's only a cape anyway."

"It's not silly; I worked very hard on that. Mum needs it to keep her shoulders warm in the mornings when she has her tea upstairs. Mummy, tell him it's not silly!" whined Jasmine.

"James, it's a very lovely bed jacket. The cape style lets me wear it over any of my gowns. Don't be bratty, or you shall spend the day in your room, and not with the others on the Hunt."

"I'm sorry, and I'm sorry to you too, Jasmine...Will you open mine now, Mummy?"

"Of course, let me put this down first." Jeanette placed the bed jacket on the table, and looked at the presents in her lap.

"The big one first, then the other one, they go together."

"That's fine, let's see what we have here..." Jeanette said as she opened the larger package. *"...It's a? A? Let me take it out and get a good look at it."*

"It's a jewelry holder. See, it's a hand, and you put it on its base like this." James took the smooth hand shaped piece of wood from his mother, and twisted it into the flat piece he removed from the wrappings. The hand stood up on the table.

"The fingers are curved so you can put your necklaces on them, and the thumb has holes for your earrings, and this shallow place in the base is for your hair combs. It's walnut, from that branch that fell from the tree behind the stables. And I made it all myself."

"Well, isn't that inventive, who showed you how to do all that." an amazed Jeanette inquired. She ran her hand over the wood, feeling how wonderfully smooth it was.

"Mikey, in the stables; He does a lot of wood stuff. He let me use his knives and files and everything. He showed me how to find the right piece of wood for what we was, I mean were making. How to make the base and the stand fit together, but still be able to come apart. This is for when you travel too. So you don't have to worry where everything gets to, it's all in one place. Isn't it super? Oh! Open the other one now!"

"All right James, calm yourself a bit, I'll open it now." Jeanette carefully opened the smaller package that was wrapped in tissue paper.

73

"Why, what a pretty Comb. Thank you James!" she exclaimed as she pulled him into a hug. "This will match the dress I'm wearing to the dance tonight. However did you know?"

"Jasmine helped me on that one. She saw it when we all went to town. She knew I was looking for something to put on the tray. I thought this was pretty, and I had some money, 'cause my gift didn't really cost anything. I'm glad you like it."

"I really do. It's wonderful, as is the jewelry stand. I still can't believe the two of you are so grown up and so talented. Come here for another hug, both of you!"

"The guests are starting to arrive," Nancy announced, as she came in to finish tidying up the room, "Mr. Groves has them by the gazebo as you requested. Your mounts are ready for you there as well."

"Thank you Nancy," said Jeanette, "The children's presents took a while longer than we'd planned this morning. Could you please see that these other lovely gifts are taken to my room, I'll have to open them later?" Jeanette gave Nancy a smile over the twins' heads, so she'd let the other staff members know why their gifts hadn't been opened or acknowledged. It wouldn't do to slight anyone. They were the best help anywhere in the county, and she wouldn't want to lose them.

Over at the gazebo there were five riders with their horses so far, with others coming up the drive. They were expecting eight to ten families, with a few single friends and older relatives. A nice sized hunt, neither too big nor too small.

Peter, the groom, had Gentry and Queenie waiting, as well as, the two ponies. All the children who were of riding age would be allowed to ride behind the adults as they ran over the fields proper. Once they arrived into the woods, and released the hounds, the "Nanny" would take the children on a shorter, easier ride, circling back to the Manor, while the adults rode after the hounds to find the fox.

It was a lovely day for a hunt. The sun was shining, the birds were singing, there was a crisp feel to the air and the leaves crackled under the horse hooves. This was exactly what Jeanette had wished for in asking for good weather. She loved the feel of Queenie, her horse, as she cantered across the fields. The strength of her, the feeling of freedom, as if she could go anywhere, be anyone. Ahhh...if only that was possible, well for a few short minutes, it was, and she enjoyed it immensely.

"So now, I'm Jeanette," Jade thinks. "I guess I should've expected this. The pattern hasn't changed in a month, why should I expect it to now. I'm an English Lady, and I'm off to the Hunt. That sure was a nice send off," she smiled.

"Well, for someone's who's never ridden a horse, this is fun. I've read enough books with hunts in them to know kind of what to expect. I wonder if I get the fox. If I'll dream about that yucky part, where they kill him? Probably the way things are going. I/she sure wanted that tail for her hat, 'How Gross' as the kids today say. Guess I'll find out next week."

For now let's see if I can hunt down that foxy hubby of mine. I must be early; I don't even hear the shower yet." Tippy-toeing into the bathroom she grabs him around the waist.

"What the hell..." is his startled response. Then he turns and gives her an evil grin. "So you're wanting to be playing this morning are you lassie," he says in a very bad Scottish accent. "Well then there's playing to be done." He gently shoves her under the showerhead and turns it on.

"You rat!" she laughs, looking like the rat herself, a drowned one. She hasn't bothered to take off her gown yet. "Two can play that game," and she pulls him into the shower with her.

Sometime later, they emerge clean and happy. The nightgown is a soggy mess on the tile floor. Jade bends over to pick it up and Jake slaps her damp bottom. "Hey, watch it. That hurts on bare skin," she pouts.

"Shall I kiss it and make it all better?" he says in a not really contrite voice.

75

"Start that and we'll both be late. Just get dressed lover boy. The Navy needs you to teach it's bright young officers about Maritime History."

"If you say so, you don't know what you're missing."

"Yes I do, and from here I can see I'm not missing much…it's colder in here that I realized. So go put your toys away for now, and we'll play later, I promise. It's not like we didn't just have a very satisfying round one, or two and three in my case." She giggles.

"I have an early appointment for a change, get dressed, so I can get my self together and get going." With that, they get ready for the day, and go off to their respective offices.

Chapter 12

Thursday
4 Oct '07

"Liebhabering? Are you awake? Johanna?" Her husband whispered in her ear as she was slowly becoming conscious. *"I'd like to give you your first birthday gift,"* he said with a twinkle in his voice.

"Not that again…Jarvis, you give me the same thing every year." She replied in mock annoyance, but couldn't stifle her laughter as he started to tickle her. Turning her gently, they'd just started to kiss when the door burst open, and two kids jumped on the bed.

"I told you she was awake." The little girl said, half-playful, half-bratty.

"But Vater said to wait until HE opened the door," replied her brother, not really whining.

"Well I guess it's too late for that now. Come on kids, lets all kiss Mutter 30 times for her 30th Geburtstag!" So saying, they all tackled Johanna and kissed her everywhere they could manage. On her face, her neck, her arms, her hands, it became a wrestling match.

"Enough! Peace! I surrender! Let me up and I'll make you all some breakfast. You two go and get dressed, and we'll be down in a bit. Jan, be my big boy and put some more coals on the fires, but don't smother them. Joselyn, please get the table ready for breakfast. Ich Liber Dich Alles!

The twins scampered out of the room, closing the door as they went. Johanna turned back to her Jarvis. "Now about that present? I think you were about to unwrap it?"

"I think I can manage to find something to amuse you Schatzi, I know you like kisses here..." He said, trailing kisses up her arm towards her throat. "And here..." now kissing behind her ears, and nibbling on her ear lobe. "And here..." covering her mouth in passion.

Jarvis was quite a kisser, each one even deeper than the last; it was like he was trying to climb inside her heart, as it was melting into his. Both sets of hands were removing clothes, and caressing warm skin. Petting and playing, while the kisses continued to evolve into a total union of breaths and souls.

Johanna cooked up breakfast wursts and potato cakes. There was kaffe and milch for das kinder. Dark brot, and butter, fresh melone, and erdbeeres, in September! "Melons and strawberries, speak English! Johanna, coffee and milk, English!" she said aloud. "The children need the English!"

"And so do I, living in the big city of New York," she thought. "I need to speak better to do my shopping." The endless supply of foods delighted her. She could find almost anything, all year round. "What a great city. To be sure, it had its problems, yet it was so good to us. Jarvis has a good job. The children go to a good school, right down the block. And the ease with which I can get all the shopping done, just great."

"Fruhstuck is ready!" she called. "I mean breakfast!"

As she walked into the dining room, Jarvis and the children shouted, "Alles gute zum Geburtstag! Happy Birthday Muter!

Right where she was planning on putting the platter of food were gaily-wrapped packages. Jarvis took the platter, "Here let me take that. You sit, and we'll serve you today." He said smiling, and placed the platter on the sideboard.

Jan pulled out her chair and Joselyn placed a ring of flowers in her hair as Johanna sat. "This is all lovely!" She said. "I wasn't expecting you to go to this much trouble."

"YOU only turn 30 once." Jarvis grinned. "You're old as me now."

"Only for 2 weeks Vater," laughed Joselyn, as Jan poured the Kaffe. "You'll be OLD again in 2 weeks"

"Thank you for that reminder kleiner madchen, I appreciate it." Jarvis picked up Joselyn and swung her around once, putting her right back in place.

"My turn," piped up Jan.

"I wouldn't forget you kleiner hosenmatz." Jarvis grabbed Jan and swung him harder, and plopped him down in his seat. "Time to eat before everything gets cold."

After the meal was cleaned up, Johanna asked to move the presents to the front room. She enjoyed sitting on the large sofa that backed to the big picture window over looking the street. How pretty the paper she had pasted on the walls was in the morning light. The two large chairs by the fireplace had been her mother's, the lace curtains his. A nice blend of the old world and this new one.

Sitting in the middle of the sofa, with one child on either side, Johanna said, "Now we are ready for the gifts!" and she started laughing.

"What is so funny muter?" asked Jan, "Why do you laugh?"

"The English, the word gift in English is to mean present. But in German, the word pronounced like gift means poison. So I said it was time for poison. There are a few of the words like that; I cannot help but to laugh.

"I think I understand, can you open whatever they are now?"

"Yes, I am ready now; let's see what surprises my lovely family has for me."

"Yes, I am   Johanna, three for three."   Jade awakes feeling somewhat comforted by the normalcy of the pattern. "At least I can understand this," she says. "Some calm in the confusion, and the food isn't bad either.' She laughs to herself. "I love breakfast wursts, and dark breads, and applekuchen. Yep! I can get into that breakfast! Now if I only had someone to make it for me."

Poor Jake is in another student meeting; the fall semester is usually the hardest one. The plebes are so afraid of their own shadows; it takes constant mentoring to get them to start thinking on their own. Surprisingly, you did want independent thought in a history class.

Jake walks in as Jade is putting dinner on the table, that's late for him.   As he sees the   Bratwursts, spaetzle, sauerkraut, green beans, and a lovely apfelkuchen, he can't help thinking, "She must have had the German dream today. Maybe that will help later."

Jade announces as they all get seated, "Tonight we are having this nice German dinner, in honor of Johanna." Then spends the rest of the meal explaining to the twins about the three dreams she keeps having, and how they are the reason for tonight's menu.

After dinner sitting side by side on the couch, watching CSI, Jake starts talking, "CAPTAIN Lewis called me into his office as I was leaving this afternoon, that's why I was late. He wanted to let me know that I'm on a short list to be assigned to---er--- England, or --- um---- Germany as a Naval Liaison Officer."

Jade twists her body around to face her husband, who is staring straight ahead, "England or Germany. Why? How soon are they talking? The semester isn't over, we'll have to sell the house, and we'll have to…"

"Hold on there, I said I am on a short list. You know that once the promotion comes through next summer, I'm being transferred somewhere. This just may come a bit early. Nothing is definite."

"OK, you just surprised me is all. Couldn't you have eased me into it?"

"How?" Jake asked, puzzled by his wife's reaction.

"I don't know, how about-'you know how you've always wanted to visit London, well we might be stationed only an hour away'." Jade giggled. Now that she's over the shock, it's almost funny. Almost. "Or 'I hear the Christmas Markets in Germany are wonderful, and we might get the chance to see them next year.'"

"So you didn't like the direct approach. Just remember that the next time you accuse me of beating around the bush. You're always saying I should just get to the point. Will you make up your mind woman?" Jake laughs with her.

"I don't have to...its a woman's prerogative to change it...often! Did he say when you'd know? How soon they are planning on choosing?"

"Lewis thinks the announcement will be out right after the first of the year. With the standard 30 days for me to report, you will follow after the house sells, and the loose ends are tied up. The Commander in Germany has a sick wife and she needs to come back here for treatment. What ever it is, it maybe serious. The Commander in England would like the position in Germany for the last two years of his tour. So whoever is selected gets their choice. If they will take England then that guy moves to Germany. If the new guy prefers Germany, then the current guy stays put in England.

So I guess the next question is what it will be, if I'm selected that is, England or Germany? I'd prefer England, the position's a better one, and you know I've always wanted to live there. But you've always said you'd like to live in Germany."

"I really don't know. I'll need some time to think about it. I understand the schools are better in England. We won't have to pay for a private one. The military schools are said to be pretty bad in Germany. We won't have to worry about the language barrier. And living an hour away from London does have a lot to say for itself. I'd probably go with you on that, but I'll need to see all the info on bases, towns, etc. You know how I am."

"Yep, and all that will wait until after the first of the year, remember I'm only one of three or four officers being considered. I think it's time to turn in, I'm wondering what a little "dry" lovemaking might be like for a change, care to find out?" Jake laughs,.

"Sounds good to me!" answers Jade, racing him up the stairs.

Chapter 13

Tuesday
9 Oct '07

She awoke slowly to the sounds of the little ones sleeping, knowing the sun was just beginning its rise. The arm around her slowly tightened as Black Hawk whispered, "Morning, my little Wolf, what do you wish on your birthing day?"

Smiling, Lilac Wolf turned to face her lover, her soul mate, her reason for being, and gently kissed him. "This is all I want. To be like this forever."

"That would spoil the kits' surprises, but if you wish..." and laughing, he rolled to her and started her morning with the softest kiss. Slowly it grew stronger, as his hands lightly caressed her ear lobes and teased her neck. Trailing kisses across her chin, he began nibbling on the sensitive lobe, and licking that lovely spot right behind it.

Lilac Wolf stretched her body so it was better lined up with his, and gave a bit of a purr. Slowly she ran her hand in circles on her Hawk's outer thigh. Softly enough to tickle... not that a great warrior could be tickled of course! As he started kissing down her throat, she started caressing up his thigh.

Hawk was kissing lower and lower, she was circling higher and higher. Both were trying to keep their moans of pleasure quiet, so the kits stayed asleep. Just as she reached that sensitive crease between leg and body,

83

he took her nipple in his mouth. She gasped with pleasure, her whole body on fire.

After a moment of pure ecstasy, her mind cleared enough to take him in her hand and run her fingers up and down the firm thickness of him. It was her turn to make him gasp. A few well-placed caresses along the top of his magnificent manhood had him more than ready to finish pleasing her. And please her he did!

They had barely finished when both kits were on top of them "The sun rises, your day is here!" The little ones exclaimed. "Are you going to stay in the furs for ever? We can see the light."

"Now Turq, you know I get this one day, to enjoy the furs until the sun is over the rivers edge. Would you have me spoil the surprise of your aunts, as they make me my birth morning meal?"

"It's not our sire's day, why does he stay in the furs?" asked Grey pup.

"It's my job to keep her warm," answered Black Hawk, with a smile for the boy, and a wink for Lilac Wolf. "It wouldn't do for her to catch a chill on this day would it?" he asked, trying to look serious.

"I guess not," said the pup, with his head hung down, "I wouldn't like that."

"I wouldn't either," piped up Turquoise chick.

"Why so glum little pup?" asked Lilac Wolf.

"I can't give you your birth gift in the tepee. Now I have to wait for the sun, and it moves so slowly," he pouted.

Black Hawk stepped into his leggings and moccasins, picked up Grey pup and carried him out of the hut.

"And you? You're being rather quiet my little chick."

"I can wait; my gift can be given any time." Turq said with a smile. She helped her mother dress in her best buckskin tunic and leggings; braid feathers into her hair; put on her necklaces of shells and beads; slip on

her moccasins; and drape a raccoon skin cape over her shoulder. Then they shook out the furs and stacked them away, setting the hut in order for the day.

Mother and daughter left the hut and walked towards the central fire, hand in hand. Others were gathering, everyone called greetings to Lilac Wolf and Turquoise chick. It was a happy, loving, family feeling that enveloped the scene in an early morning mist. The fire was blazing with many cook pots around it. Blankets and furs had been spread around the sunny end of the clearing. All the children were running and playing as if this was a holiday.

Lilac Wolf looked around her. They were a small village of Catawba, only seven hands of huts, in half circles on the west edge of the Iswa river. The sweat lodge was to the north, and the woman's lodge way off to the south. Small fields now lay fallow, just past the edge of the village; the sun was shining on the water, as it slowly passed the horizon.

She said a silent prayer of thanks to "He who Never Dies", then joined her family for the celebration. She was led to a place of honor and seated on a large bearskin. Her sister brought her a bowl of apples and nuts to start the meal. An aunt served a mash of squash and corn with honey in it, and some roasted rabbit from a morning kill. The morning beverage of herbs was warm and spicy as Turquoise chick handed her a small cup.

Once she was served, everyone else went to the pots to get their food. The Braves ate first, or at least were served first. Then came the boys, next were the mothers, with the maidens and little girls last in line. Today the order made no real difference, there was plenty of food for all, but in the dead of winter it could be crucial. Everyone sat around and talked as they ate. The dogs wandered around looking for handouts, children slipped them bites when they thought no one was looking, and the adults ignored it, in the spirit of celebration.

When the eating was finished, Great Eagle, the Medicine Man, stood to begin the blessings of the day. He'd barely started when the sentries shouted alarm, "The Cherokee Come!"

85

Everyone scattered screaming, mothers grabbing children, running for their huts. Warriors were looking for their bows and running for their horses. The enemy was upon them before Lilac Wolf's people could protect themselves. She had almost gotten into her hut, had just pushed the children to safety, when a Cherokee Brave rode right over her. The horse knocked her on her back, and stepped on her chest with his hind leg. The Brave never saw Lilac Wolf. It only took a moment.

Lilac Wolf got half a scream out. Once the horse was past, the kits ran to her crying, "Don't die, don't die!" Turq cradled her head, as Grey held her hand sobbing. Black Hawk was there as if by magic.

She looked up at them and murmured "Beware 30...must warn next!" And faded away.

"Wait!" screams Jade as she wakes with a start. Sitting bolt upright in her bed, eyes wide open, seeing nothing. "You can't die...what does it mean?"

Jake comes running into the room, "What's wrong? Are you ok? Are you hurt?" It takes him a moment to realize she's not really seeing him, or talking to him. "Gently he sits down on the bed and draws her into his arms.

"Its ok. hun...what ever it is, it's gone now. I have you...you're safe."

"It was...I was...She was..." Jade sobs as she buries her face in Jake's chest. He just holds her until she stops crying. Once she can catch her breath, Jade smiles at Jake and gives him a kiss.

"I don't know what I'd do without you," she says weakly.

"Well, you don't have to worry about that now do you? Do you want to talk about it, or are you better off just letting it go for now and we can chat about it later?"

"I think I'm ok now. Lilac Wolf died...was killed.

She's the Catawba woman I've been dreaming about," she adds at Jakes confused look. "I was her. The Cherokee raided the village, and a horse trampled me. I saved the kids, almost got to my hut. The horse and rider came around the hut and just rode right over me. He never saw me, just mowed me down.

The kits came screaming out of the hut, I was barely alive, as they held me I said, Beware 30...must warn next," Jade shudders. "What can it mean? I mean I was HER! Am I going crazy? It's only a month until my birthday. Is she trying to tell me something? If so what? I can't take any more of this!"

"Hush now," Jake coos, "I'm here. I'm sure it's nothing to be worried about, just too much going at work and the worry about us being transferred. Think about it, where are the two places they are likely to send us? Germany and England?"

"Yeah, but I started the dreams before we knew about that. A full month before. Maybe I'm psychic. We both know I'm psycho," she tries to joke. Her laugh comes out strained, but it's a start.

"Do you want me to stay awhile? I have that senior this week, doing the leadership course. All I'm doing is sitting in the back of the class and watching him anyway," Jake offers.

"No, I'm all right now, or at least better. I'll just sit here a bit longer to get myself together and then get my shower. Can you get the kids off to school? I don't want to have to put on a front for them. The thought feels like too much work. You know how good Jen is at seeing right through me. I think she's part gypsy or something."

This time the smile is real, and she's feeling calmer. "I'm not opening today, so I have some time," she says, as Jake gives her a kiss and goes down to deal with the twins.

Once everyone else is gone, Jade gets out of bed and takes her shower. It's silly to feel safer in an empty house, than one with her family in it. She is worried about her mental health, is she really losing it? Or are the women real? Why is she resisting that thought so strongly? Is that what the Hawk poem had really been about?

87

When the hot water starts to run out, Jade finally steps out of the shower, dries off and gets dressed. As she enters the kitchen, she finds that Jake has left her a pot of coffee. "Now there's a real sweetie," she thinks. "Making that coffee just for me." She knows he always stops by the WaWa at the end of the street for his cup of Hazelnut and a breakfast sandwich.

She gets the Hawk poem from her briefcase and rereads it as she sips her coffee. "Why do you Hesitate? Why do you Doubt? All is in you…Believe!" Jade reads that verse aloud.

"What am I susposed to believe? That I'm suddenly psychic? Do I really even believe in that? For other people sure, but not for me. Do I believe that I can dream about ghosts? Nope! Not possible, I'm the least psychic person I know, unless you were talking about Jake or the kids. Then maybe there is a bit of ESP hanging around, but that's only because I know them so well.

This just isn't making any sense. Maybe instead of looking to the poem for answers, I should call one of those psychic hotline numbers. Bet this isn't a question they get every day. "'Are the re-occurring dreams I've been having about these three women on their thirtieth birthdays really just figments of my imagination? Am I dreaming about spirits from beyond the veil? Or have I lost my mind?' It's almost worth the money for the reactions."

With her coffee finished, Jade rinses her cup and gathers her things. It's time to get to work and put this back into the far corner of her mind for the rest of the day.

Chapter 14

Wednesday
10 Oct '07

"Surprise, Mummy!" The twins laughed as they climbed on the big four-poster bed, "We got you presents and Pappa is having Cook make a fancy breakfast even though it isn't Sunday, all because it's your birthday." Their voices were so jumbled together it was hard to tell who was saying what.

"Children, calm yourselves, please." Jeanette said while trying to gather them in a big hug. Looking towards the doorway, she saw Jackson standing there laughing.

"Well, you might help, you know?" She laughed.

"And spoil all their fun? Would I do that, Jeanee?" was his reply. He came into the room scooping up James, as Jeanette managed to grab onto Jasmine.

"You two need to let your mother finish waking up and get dressed, if you want to have that fancy breakfast." Jack said to the children, in a fake stern voice.

"Yes, Sir!" they both replied together, trying not to laugh. Jack set down James as Jeanette let go of Jasmine, and the kids ran from the room. With a wink and a smile, Jack closed the door after them and returned to the bed.

"May I help you with your nightclothes?" He asked, untying her nightgown as he kissed her.

"But, Sir! What will the servants think?" Jeanette asked in a mockingly shocked voice.

"Whatever I pay them to think. Or in this case, what I pay them NOT to think!" He laughed. "Jeanee, you're so beautiful, I'm the luckiest man in England, Europe, the whole world!"

Kissing, they fell back together. Slowly Jackson unbuttoned the gown that Jeanette wore, one button at a time, kissing the bared skin as he went. He usually hated these high-necked styles, but this was fun. Under the chin...on the throat...that cute little cleft where the collarbones meet...where her locket hangs...at the top of her cleavage...deep in the middle...at the bottom. This could take hours, as he leisurely drew circles along the edges of her breasts.

Jeanette let out a low moan. She had been trying to pretend indifference, being still, with a haughty look on her face. A woman could only resist so much. Every nerve she had was tingling. She knew it wasn't "lady like" but she finally took his head and moved it to one exposed breast and said softly "Please!"

That's all he'd been waiting for; he lifted Jeanette up enough to remove her gown the rest of the way. "I want to see all of you," he murmured, caressing her body. "You keep getting more beautiful, even more beautiful that when we first met. More beautiful than you were last year." He started kissing all those places he had been caressing, starting back at her breasts, slowly circling to her navel, and then softly moving lower....

Walking down the stairs, Jeanette turned to Jackson and said, "I had the strangest dream last night. It was about one of those Colonial Natives. It was as if I were her or something. I was seeing out of her eyes as her birthday celebration took place. It was very creepy. Then she died; she was run over by another savage on his horse. She said the oddest thing: "Beware 30...must warn the next."

"How very strange" replied Jack, "must have been all of Christopher's talking about his exploits over there during his visit."

"I would think so; it was certainly unsettling. I will not let it ruin the hunt, and I did manage to block it out for a while there," she smiled at him, "yet it lingers."

Entering into the breakfast room, painted in creams and yellows to accent the easterly facing windows, Jeanette and Jackson were in full hunting regalia.

"Oh, look! Mummy has on her new boots. I told you Pappa would give them to her before they came down," came Jasmine's very grown up comment.

"I thought so too," said James, "I'm just not bragging about it. Look at all your presents Mummy. These two are from me!"

"Everything looks wonderful. Those two look perfect James. I bet you wrapped them yourself as well." She laughed, as she saw the slightly mangled cloth on the larger one. It's odd shape making it difficult for an adult to wrap properly, and impossible for a 10 year old to manage. The smaller package was much neater, if you ignored the ink smudge, and the knots in the ribbon.

"How did you know?" James asked, looking rather confused in that little boy way.

"Just look at it, anyone can tell," sniped Jasmine.

"That wasn't very nice." David said. "Boys his age aren't as artistic as girls are."

"Yeah! But I can run faster than you, and I can fish better too...so there!" James snapped.

Just as things were about to get heated between the kids, Dolly, the cook, came in carrying a big platter of eggs and sausages. Sally, the scullery maid, followed carrying bacon, and biscuits, and puddings, and pastries, all the makings of a Fancy breakfast. Nancy came over to pour the tea, and serve the meal. Having been with the family for over 5 years now she knew exactly what every one wanted. She was the best downstairs maid they'd ever had, almost like part of the family.

91

Conversation during the meal centered on the Birthday hunt. Who would be here, who couldn't make it and why. Which children were likely to attend, and how far they would be allowed to ride with the Hunt. Who would be Nanny this year? If Uncle Milton would be thrown by his horse this year? Always a great topic for discussion.

After the dishes had been cleared and the tea had been refreshed, the children each picked up their presents and stood in front of their mother.

"Oh my, well who should go first?" Jeanette asked.

"I should, me! Me!" said James, jumping up and down. "I'm oldest!"

"BY only 5 minutes," replied Jasmine. "And you went first last year."

"Did Not!" whined James

"Yes you did, with that blue scarf you gave her. I remember," was Jasmine's answer.

"Oh, yeah...then I guess it's your turn. Well hurry up. You're taking too long."

"Here mum, I made this all by my self. It's why I've been in my room reading so much lately."

"Why thank you Jasmine. What pretty paper, where did you find it?" Jeanette asked.

"Pappa took us into town with him last week when you went to see Aunt Susan. It was all a big surprise." Jasmine giggled. "Open it!"

Carefully, Jeanette opened the package and found a knitted bed jacket all done in light blues and greens, with a purple ribbon tie. "My! This is beautiful. Where did you learn to knit something this light and dainty? Not from me, that's for sure."

"It's actually crochet, and Sally taught me. It's really quite simple, once you have the right needle and the right thin yarns. That was the hard

92

part. Trying to explain to Pappa what I needed when he went to town last month. But he did real well," she said in a very adult tone.

"Yes I can see that. And so did you! I'm very proud of you. This is so very soft. I can't wait to wear it tomorrow morning. Come here so I can give you a big hug." Jeanette moved her chair away from the table so she could embrace her daughter.

"My turn now!" James said as he pushed his present between his mother and sister. I made you something you really need. Not some silly old bed jacket. It's only a cape anyway."

"It's not silly; I worked very hard on that. Mum needs it to keep her shoulders warm in the mornings when she has her tea up stairs. Mummy, tell him it's not silly!" whined Jasmine.

"James it's a very lovely bed jacket. The cape style lets me wear it over any of my gowns. Don't be bratty, or you shall spend the day in your room, and not with the others on the Hunt."

"I'm sorry, and I'm sorry to you too Jasmine…Will you open mine now Mummy?"

"Of course, let me put this down first." Jeanette placed the bed jacket on the table, and looked at the presents in her lap.

"The big one first, then the other one, they go together."

"That's fine, let's see what we have here…" Jasmine said as she opened the larger package. "…It's a? A? Let me take it out and get a good look at it."

"It a Jewelry holder. See, it's a hand, and you put it on its base like this." James took the smooth wooden hand shaped piece of wood from his mother, and twisted it into the flat piece he removed from the wrappings. The hand stood up on the table.

"The fingers are curved so you can put your necklaces on them, and the thumb has holes for your earrings. And this shallow place in the base is for your hair combs. It's walnut, from that branch that fell from the tree behind the stables. And I made it all myself."

93

"Well, isn't that inventive, who showed you how to do all that?" An amazed Jeanette inquired. She ran her hand over the wood, feeling how wonderfully smooth it was.

"Mikey, in the stables. He does a lot of wood stuff. He let me use his knives and files and everything. He showed me how to find the right piece of wood for what we was, I mean were making. How to make the base and the stand fit together, but still be able to come apart. This is for when you travel too. So you don't have to worry where everything gets to, it's all in one place. Isn't it super? Oh! Open the other one now!"

"All right James, calm yourself a bit, I'll open it now." Jeanette carefully opened the smaller package that was wrapped in tissue paper. "Why, what a pretty Comb. Thank you James!" she exclaimed as she pulled him into a hug. "This will match the dress I'm wearing to the dance tonight. However did you know?"

"Jasmine helped me on that one. She saw it when we all went to town. She knew I was looking for something to put on the tray. I thought this was pretty, and I had some money, 'cause my gift didn't cost. I'm glad you like it."

"I really do. It's wonderful, as is the jewelry stand. I still can't believe the two of you are so grown up and so talented. Come here for another hug, both of you!"

"The guests are starting to arrive," Nancy announced, as she came in to finish tidying up the room, "Mr. Groves has them by the gazebo as you requested. Your mounts are ready for you there as well."

"Thank you Nancy," said Jeanette, "The children's presents took a while longer than we'd planned this morning. Could you please see that these other lovely gifts are taken to my room, I'll have to open them later." Jeanette gave Nancy a smile over the twins' heads, so she'd let the other staff members know why their gifts hadn't been opened or acknowledged. It wouldn't do to slight anyone. They were the best help anywhere in the county, and she wouldn't want to lose them.

Over at the gazebo there were five riders with their horses so far, with others coming up the drive. They were expecting eight to ten families, with a few single friends and older relatives. A nice sized hunt, neither too big nor too small. Peter, the groom, had Gentry and Queenie waiting, as well as, the two ponies.

All the children who were of riding age were allowed to ride behind the adults as they ran over the fields proper. Once they arrived into the woods, and released the hounds, the "Nanny" took the children on a shorter, easier ride, circling back to the Manor, while the adults rode after the hounds to find the fox.

It was a lovely day for a hunt. The sun was shining, the birds were singing, there was a crisp feel to the air and the leaves crackled under the horse hooves. This was exactly what Jeanette had wished for in asking for good weather. She loved the feel of Queenie, her horse, as she cantered across the fields. The strength of her, the feeling of freedom, as if she could go anywhere, be anyone. Ahhh...if only that was possible, well for a few short minutes, it was, and she enjoyed it immensely.

The fox made a dash out of the trees and across a corner of the Peterson's cornfield with the hounds right behind, baying out their song. The hunters moved to canter as they came to open ground, enjoying the faster pace after all the time walking through the trees. It wasn't a large field, so they didn't get up much speed as they came to a large tree over a brook on the edge of an apple orchard. The fox was giving them quite a merry chase. Half of the hunters swerved off to the right, to go the long way around the orchard. The other half jumped the log and continued up the path through the middle after the dogs

.----------

"How strange," is Jades first thought as she becomes conscious this morning, "how can Jeanette have a dream about Lilac Wolf? Why would she? This doesn't make any sense." She starts to laugh.

"Make sense...right! Like any of this does. That was a good one Jade!" she says aloud, still chuckling to her self as she's walking towards the bathroom.

"Did you say something?" asks Jake, poking his head out of the shower. "What's so funny? Come on in and share the joke."

"I am on my way." Jade climbs in beside him and begins to explain, why it's so funny. "It doesn't make sense for Jeanette to have a dream about Lilac Wolf," she tells Jake. "How can one of my dreams know about the other one? It's as if I have Multiple Personality Disorder and the alter's are beginning to find out about each other. I wonder if they'll integrate," she laughs again.

Jake just stands in the running water, looking at her quizzically, nodding his head as if he understands every word, but not getting a thing she says. Finally, Jade just gives him a big kiss. It doesn't really matter if he understands. She does, and the kiss is turning into more; she turns her mind off and turns Jake's body on.

"Jake's body," Jade muses, "now that is a subject she can spend hours thinking about. Six feet of lean, mean, loving machine!" She chuckles at that thought. "Those baby blue eyes, that dark curly hair, I wish the Navy would let him grow it longer. I love the way it wants to curl up in the back. I used to enjoy playing with it, back when he was allowed to have some.

Then there is that body, Mmm! One good thing about the military is it keeps a man in shape. A woman too, of course, but I'm only interested in one man, mine." Smiling she continues her drive into work, daydreaming about her husbands body.

Chapter 15

Thursday
11 Oct '07

"Liebhabering? Are you awake? Johanna?" Her husband whispered in her ear as she was slowly becoming conscious. *"I'd like to give you your first birthday gift,"* he said with a twinkle in his voice.

"Not that again...Jarvis, you give me the same thing every year." She replied in mock annoyance, but couldn't stifle her laughter as he started to tickle her. Turning her gently, they'd just started to kiss when the door burst open, and two kids jumped on the bed.

"I told you she was awake." The little girl said, half-playful, half-bratty.

"But Vater said to wait until HE opened the door," replied her brother, not really whining.

"Well I guess it's too late for that now. Come on kids, lets all kiss Mutter 30 times for her 30th Geburtstag!" So saying, they all tackled Johanna and kissed her everywhere they could manage. On her face, her neck, her arms, her hands; it became a wrestling match.

"Enough! Peace! I surrender! Let me up and I'll make you all some breakfast. You two go and get dressed, and we'll be down in a bit. Jan, be my big boy and put some more coals on the fires, but don't smother them. Joselyn, please get the table ready for breakfast. Ich Liber Dich Alles!"

*The twins scampered out of the room, closing the door as they went .
Johanna turned back to her Jarvis. "Now about that present? I think
you were about to unwrap it?"*

*"I think I can manage to find something to amuse you Schatzi, I know
you like kisses here..." He said, trailing kisses up her arm towards her
throat. "And here..." now kissing behind her ears, and nibbling on her
ear lobes, "and here..." covering her mouth in a passionate kiss.*

*Jarvis was quite a kisser, each one even deeper than the last; it was as if
he was trying to climb inside her heart, as it was melting into his. Both
sets of hands were removing clothes, and caressing warm skin. Petting
and playing, while the kisses continued to evolve into a total union of
breaths and souls. Eventually the kisses started traveling to other body
parts, after all everything tasted so good. And taste they did, from their
nose to their toes, and various favorite spots in between.*

*Johanna cooked up wursts, and potato cakes. There was kaffe and
milch for das kinder. Dark brot, and butter, fresh melone, and
erdbeeres, in September! "Melons and strawberries, speak English!
Johanna, coffee and milk, English!" she said aloud. "The children
need the English!"*

*"And so do I, living in the big city of New York," she thought. "I need
to speak better to do my shopping." The endless supply of foods
delighted her in New York. She could find almost anything, all year
round. "What a great city. To be sure, it had its problems, yet it was so
good to us. Jarvis has a good job. The children go to a good school,
right down the block. And the ease with which I can get all the
shopping done, just great."*

"Fruhstuck is ready!" She called. "I mean breakfast!"

*As she walked into the dining room, Jarvis and the children shouted
"Alles Gute Zum Geburtstag! Happy Birthday Muter!*

*Right where she had planned to place the platter of food were gaily-
wrapped packages. Jarvis took the platter, "Here let me take that. You
sit, and we'll serve you today." He said smiling, and placed the platter
on the sideboard.*

Jan pulled out her chair and Joselyn placed a ring of flowers in her hair as Johanna sat. "This is all lovely!" She said. "I wasn't expecting you to go to this much trouble."

"YOU only turn 30 once." Jarvis grinned. "You're old as me now."

"Only for 2 weeks Vater." Joselyn laughed, as Jan poured the Kaffe. "You'll be OLD again in 2 weeks"

"Thank you for that reminder kleiner madchen, I appreciate it." Jarvis picked up Joselyn and swung her around once, putting her right back in place.

"My turn," piped up Jan.

"I wouldn't forget you kleiner hosenmatz." Jarvis grabbed Jan and swung him harder, and plopped him down in his seat. "Time to eat before everything gets cold."

As they were eating Johanna said quietly to Jarvis " I had a strange dream last night. About an Indian frau who was also having a birthday, but a bad Indian came and ran over her with his horse.

It was very confusing. I didn't much like it. To awaken was a good thing this morgen. And the help in the awakening was good as well."

Jarvis blushed a bit and replied, "Watch what you say, you know they can hear, but the dream does sound strange. Maybe from the books you are reading, about the settlers? One cannot know these things. We need to finish eating the good food you made, there are many surprises on this day."

After the meal was cleaned up, Johanna asked to move the presents to the front room. She enjoyed sitting on the large sofa that backed to the big picture window overlooking the street. How pretty the paper she had pasted on the walls was in the morning light. The two large chairs by the fireplace were her mothers, the lace curtains his. A nice blend of the old world and this new one.

Sitting in the middle of the sofa, with one child on either side, Johanna said, "Now we are ready for the gifts!" and she started laughing.

"What is so funny muter?" asked Jan, "Why do you laugh?"

"The English, the word gift in English is to mean present. In German, the word pronounced like gift means poison. So I said it was time for poison. There are a few of the words like that; I cannot help but to laugh.

"I think I understand, can you open whatever they are now?"

"Yes, I am ready; let's see what surprises my lovely family has for me."

"Jan may be first," said Joselyn, "I went first last year."

"How do you remember?" asked Jan as he handed his mother a prettily wrapped box.

"I just do, I think it comes from being older," she laughed, "mostly from being a girl."

Johanna opened her gift to find a nice rectangular box with a carved lid. "My, how pretty, where did you get this?" She asked.

"I made it for you," answered Jan with pride. "Vater has been showing me how to carve the top. In school I took the class. I made the box. I hope you use it for your jewelry. I know you have some cloth to line it with. I just didn't know how to do it.

"I will do that. It is very lovely Jan, thank you so much. Come give me a kiss." Johanna hugged and kissed her son with much pride showing on her face.

"Well if Jeanette can dream about Lilac Wolf, I guess Johanna can," Jade thinks as she wakes this morning. "This everything in threes thingy is getting to be way too much. Are they going to start dressing alike? Am I ever going to have a normal dream again?

I guess it's OK knowing what you're going to dream about every Monday, Tuesday and Wednesday night. Kind of like having, TV Guide for my dreams and no one else has died. Is a whole week of non-dreams too much to ask for? Or at least the ones you don't remember, the normal ones. I can only hope," and with that she gets up and starts her day. Once again alone.

Jake's morning meetings are getting way out of hand this term. They've never been this bad before. The new department chief has started rotating mandatory weekly staff meetings. Therefore, no one would miss his or her first hour class more than once a month.

He'd tried to make it a lunch meeting but was shot down when he discovered lunches are staggered by year group. So depending on what you are teaching, you might or might not be available. No one is available for after school meetings. Most officers assisted in a sport or club activity, and didn't have the time.

That left mornings, and not being a very happy morning person, he doesn't want to come in any earlier than he has to, so first hour it is. This leaves Jake having to go in early to be sure the day's assistant knows what they are to do. Add that to the student's needs and the shower sessions, the poor baby isn't getting to sleep in any more.

When Jade arrives at work this morning she discovers a message from Alice saying that the sisters would be in a bit late as Alicia isn't feeling well and she is taking her to the doctor. This has Jade concerned; usually Alice just calls her at home. The answering machine didn't have a time stamp, so she has no way to know when the call was placed.

She debates calling Alice's cell phone to find out what's wrong. Working for the two Ladies for three and a half years makes them more than just employers. They're friends and in many ways family.

Yet she knows that if Alice really needs her she'll call, and the cell phone will probably be turned off in the doctor's office anyway. She will be a good girl and wait until Alice shows up. Waiting is not one of Jade's favorite things.

She has completed every mundane daily task she can think of when Alice finally shows up at 11:30. There have been no walk in customers, and no client appointments were scheduled for the morning. Jade has had to work to just keep herself busy while she tried not to worry.

It takes every ounce of strength not to pounce on Alice the minute she hears her key in the back door. Instead, Jade sits at her desk looking busy giving Alice time to put her stuff away and get a cup of coffee. Once she came out of the back office and sat at her desk Jade asks as casually as possible, "How is Alicia?"

"She's not so good," is Alice's tired reply. "She woke up at 3:30 this morning with a high fever, dizziness and vomiting, and we couldn't get it to stop. Finally around 5, I took her to the Emergency Room. They gave her fluids and medicine to slow everything down. Once her doctor came in he decided to keep her for the day to run some tests."

"What are they looking for? Do they have any idea?" asks a concerned Jade.

"They said something about an inner ear infection or vertigo. It didn't seem to be a major concern, but she is over 50 now, so they wanted to do a few scans. They were going to do a brain scan to rule out any tumor, that sort of thing. The Doctor emphasized it was only to be safe, that he really didn't think that was the problem. He thinks that the cold she had last week settled in her ear and has irritated the nerve. So I'm not worried...yet. Not unless they find something nasty in all the blood work or on the brain scan."

"Well it sounds like you did exactly the right thing in taking her in.," replies Jade, trying to sound supportive. "I know she put up a fight about going to the ER."

"No she didn't, that's what scared me the most. It was her suggestion. I was being delicate, she was doing more then just vomiting, things were leaving from both ends if you get my meaning. She was so weak; she couldn't even stand by herself. After we arrived and they were taking her history she admitted that it started over two hours before she woke me up. The poor dear, she just kept hoping it would stop. That she would run out of fluids to emit."

"Well you don't have to worry about the agency, I have no problem working to close today and filling in tomorrow too. I know you can't do it alone, especially if you're worried about Alicia."

"Thank you Jade!" a very relieved Alice says as she comes over and gives her a hug. "I don't know how we ever got so lucky to find you, or what we'll do when you're gone. You've been the best friend we've ever had, and a damn good employee too."

"Thanks," says Jade as she returns the hug. "I feel the same way too. I've been so lucky to work here. It's been like working with family, not working at a job.

Speaking of work, let me give you a run down of what I've already done this morning." The two women put their worries on hold and get on with the day's business.

Chapter 16

She awoke slowly to the sounds of the little ones sleeping, knowing the sun was just beginning its rise. The arm around her slowly tightened as Black Hawk whispered, "morning, my little Wolf, what do you wish on your birthing day?"

Smiling, Lilac Wolf turned to face her lover, her soul mate, her reason for being, and gently kissed him. "This is all I want. To be like this forever."

"That would spoil the kits' surprises, but if you wish..." and laughing, he rolled to her and started her morning with the softest kiss. Slowly it grew stronger, as his hands lightly caressed her ear lobes and teased her neck. Trailing kisses across her chin, he began nibbling on the sensitive lobe, and licking that lovely spot right behind it.

Lilac Wolf stretched her body so it was better lined up with his, and gave a bit of a purr. Slowly she ran her hand in circles on her Hawk's outer thigh. Softly enough to tickle... not that a great warrior could be tickled of course! As he started kissing down her throat, she started caressing up his thigh.

Hawk was kissing lower and lower, she was circling higher and higher. Both were trying to keep their moans of pleasure quiet, so the kits stayed asleep. Just as she reached that sensitive crease between leg and body,

*he took her nipple in his mouth. She gasped with pleasure, her whole
body on fire.*

*After a moment of pure ecstasy, her mind cleared enough to take him in
her hand and run her fingers up and down the firm thickness of him. It
was her turn to make him gasp. A few well-placed caresses along the
top of his magnificent manhood had him more than ready to finish
pleasing her. And please her he did!*

*They had barely finished when both kits were on top of them "The sun
rises, your day is here!" The little ones exclaimed. "Are you going to
stay in the furs for ever? We can see the light."*

*"Now Turq, you know I get this one day, to enjoy the furs until the sun
is over the rivers edge. Would you have me spoil the surprise of your
aunts, as they make me my birth morning meal?"*

"It's not our sire's day, why does he stay in the furs?" asked Grey pup.

*"It's my job to keep her warm," answered Black Hawk, with a smile for
the boy, and a wink for Lilac Wolf. "It wouldn't do for her to catch a
chill on this day would it?" he asked, trying to look serious.*

*"I guess not," said the pup, with his head hung down, "I wouldn't like
that."*

"I wouldn't either," piped up Turquoise chick.

"Why so glum little pup?" asked Lilac Wolf.

*"I can't give you your birth gift in the tepee. Now I have to wait for the
sun, and it moves so slowly," he pouted.*

*Black Hawk stepped into his leggings and moccasins, picked up Grey
pup and carried him out of the hut.*

"And you? You're being rather quiet my little chick."

*"I can wait; my gift can be given any time." Turq said with a smile. She
helped her mother dress in her best buckskin tunic and leggings; braid
feathers into her hair; put on her necklaces of shells and beads; slip on*

her moccasins; and drape a raccoon skin cape over her shoulder. Then they shook out the furs and stacked them away, setting the hut in order for the day.

Mother and daughter left the hut and walked towards the central fire, hand in hand. Others were gathering, everyone called greetings to Lilac Wolf and Turquoise chick. It was a happy, loving, family feeling that enveloped the scene in an early morning mist. The fire was blazing with many cook pots around it. Blankets and furs had been spread around the sunny end of the clearing. All the children were running and playing as if this was a holiday.

Thirty summers, thought Lilac Wolf, where did it all go? I feel as young as Turquoise and Grey, yet I'm to be entering the elder woman's counsel this night. I start my year of trial. Am I ready? Can I really lead the women? Can I stand up to the men? I don't feel all that wise today. Will I be in only 1 year? It seems so long and yet so short. How is this possible? Why have I been so blessed?

Lilac Wolf looked around her. They were a small village of Catawba, only seven hands of huts, in rough circles on the west edge of the Iswa river. The long house facing the water and the morning sun with the ceremonial fire in the clearing before it. The sweat lodge was to the north, and the woman's lodge way off to the south. All surrounded by young tree trunks dug into the earth to form a barrier.

One opening was easier to defend, from their enemies and from the bears that liked to raid their camp. Small fields now lay fallow, just past the edge of the village; the sun was shining on the water, as it slowly passed the horizon.

She said a silent prayer of thanks to "He who Never Dies", then joined her family for the celebration. She was led to a place of honor and seated on a large bearskin. Her sister brought her a bowl of apples and nuts to start the meal. An aunt served a mash of squash and corn with honey in it, and some roasted rabbit from this morning's kill. The tea like beverage of herbs was warm and spicy as Turquoise chick handed her a small cup.

Once she was served, everyone else went to the pots to get their food. The Braves ate first, or at least were served first. Then came the boys,

107

next were the mothers, with the maidens and little girls, last in line. Today the order made no real difference, there was plenty of food for all, but in the dead of winter, it could be crucial.

They sat around and talked as they ate. The dogs wandered looking for handouts, children slipped them bites when they thought no one was looking, and the adults ignored it, in the spirit of celebration.

When the eating was finished, Great Eagle, the Medicine Man, stood to begin the blessings of the day. He'd barely started when the sentries shouted alarm, "The Cherokee Come!"

Everyone scattered screaming, mothers grabbing children, running for their huts. Warriors were looking for their bows and running for their horses. The enemy was upon them before Lilac Wolf's people could protect themselves.

She had almost gotten into her hut, had just pushed the children to safety, when a Cherokee Brave rode right over her. The horse knocked her on her back, and stepped on her chest with his hind leg. The Brave never saw Lilac Wolf. It only took a moment.

She got out got half a scream. Once the horse was past, the kits ran to her crying, "Don't die, don't die!" Turq cradled her head, as Grey held her hand sobbing. Black Hawk was there as if by magic.

She looked up at them and murmured "Beware 30...must warn next!" And faded away.

"Ok! I'm Ok! It's just the dream!" Jade tells her self as she wakes up shaking. "It's not me, I'm alive. I'm in my bed, all safe and sound." She looks around at the softly painted walls and the picture of her parents on her dresser. "See Mom and Dad are watching over me, nothing is going to happen to me here. I'm fine. I just need a shower to clear my head, and I'll be all-better. Yeah, that's what I need, a shower, a good hot shower."

"Why does a shower always solve my problems?" She wonders as she collects her favorite towels, and gets out the new shampoo and conditioner she bought last week. "What was it about steaming, hot water flowing over you that sets everything straight? Don't really know, but I'm glad I live now when I can have one," and in she goes!

"May I help you?" asks Alice, when David enters the agency.

"I'm looking for Jade; she's working on a trip for me. I'm David Geddes."

"I'll be happy to get her, she's just in the back making a copy. Please have a seat at her desk." Alice points to a chair at Jade's desk, and goes to tell her she has a client.

"Dave, what a pleasant surprise, how may I help you today?" asks Jade as she enters the room carrying a client file, and a few photocopies. "Has something come up about your trip? Any more questions from your sister?"

"Actually, I have some information for you. I've been doing some research on your Catawba Tribe and wanted to drop off what I'd found out so far. There's more info on the Internet than I expected. But nothing as detailed as what you've given me. I printed out what I thought would interest you, and listed the most helpful of the web sites as well."

"Dave, that's very sweet of you. I guess I should have called you last week, Lilac Wolf died. She was run over by a Cherokee brave when they raided the village. She saved the children, but the horse went right over her, it was really creepy, I felt like I was her. I just wasn't up to talking about it."

"Wow that must have really scared you. That's one of the things I found out; the Catawba were on the British side of the French and Indian Wars. They were enemies with the Cherokee, and the Sioux. The tribes were constantly raiding each other. These were the scalping, counting coup sorts of Indians. But she was only a squaw, her scalp wouldn't have mattered."

"She said something odd as she died, 'Beware 30...must warn next'. Do you know anything about their curses? It doesn't sound like one to me.

It's just she was very urgent, and staring directly at me. And this is hard to do, because by then, I'd taken her place in the dreams. I was her, no shadow, or ghost. I felt everything she did, to include the pain of her death. It was all pretty bizarre."

"Sounds like it," says David a bit awed. "I've never heard anything like what you're describing. But I'll check into it. Let me know if there are any other changes. This is so intriguing; I've never known someone who was channeling a spirit before."

"Do you really think that's what I'm doing, channeling her spirit? I've thought I might be dreaming about ghosts but only as a joke, I hadn't really considered channeling a spirit. That's eerie. I wonder if I'm channeling the other two, as well."

"Other two? Have you been having dreams about two other squaws and you haven't told me? David asks indignantly.

"No, not Indians, excuse me Native Americans. One is an English lady from around the 1800's, and one is a German immigrant in N.Y. City, around the turn of the last century. The dreams follow the same patterns, and they are always on the same days in the same order. Well I guess that would follow, wouldn't it?

On Tuesday it's Lilac Wolf; on Wednesday it's Jeanette, the English lady; on Thursday it's Johanna, the German mother. They all have twins, a girl and a boy, just like I do.

We all seem to have late fall birthdays. It appears to be late October or early November in the dreams. My birthday is November 11th. I don't know if there's a connection with that or not."

"Wow, yeah, that sounds like channeling spirits to me. You should go see a psychic. Someone who can help you with all these spirits. I can't imagine going through something like this alone," David says amazed.

"My husband has been great, and the kids really help, they keep things real. Plus working here keeps me busy enough, I don't dwell on it a whole lot. But yeah, it can be rather overwhelming at times. Like the morning Lilac Wolf died. I totally wigged out. Poor Jake had quite a time trying to put me back together. He knows me so well, he knew just what to do, and I survived. That's all that really matters."

"I guess. Well, St. John's calls. I'm glad you were in so I could explain the materials in person. I know it sounds funny, but I'm sorry for your loss. I'll let you know about anything else I find." David rises shaking Jade's hand. "You keep me informed too, ok?"

"Of course, not a problem. I really do appreciate all the information you've brought me. I'm sorry for not telling you about Lilac Wolf sooner. I'll let you know if there are any more changes about her. This is just so crazy, it's hard to know what to believe and what to try to ignore," Jade says as they walk to the door. "Thanks again for stopping by."

Later that evening, Jade is in the family room reading the papers David gave her when Jake walks in. "You know how you've always liked London?" he queries.

"Are you trying to tell me something?" she asks, looking at him over her reading glasses.

"Just that two of the other officers under consideration for the posting have been withdrawn. It's now down to only me and one other guy. I don't know who he is; CAPT. Lewis hasn't been able to find out. But I wanted you to know that the odds have changed considerably. I don't want to worry you. But you have a right to know."

"Thanks Jake, I appreciate the heads up. I guess we'll deal with it if and when it happens. Look at all the information David found for me on Lilac Wolf's tribe. They are from the northern end of what is now South Carolina. And there is still a Catawba city and river. She is real. Or rather her people were. So I guess she could be too. He suggested that I was actually channeling spirits, not just having dreams. What do you think about that idea?" she asks hesitantly.

"I wouldn't have ever thought of that, but then I wasn't raised to believe in such things," answers Jake, as he gives the idea some thought. "I can see where that might make sense. They are all trying to show you something. It's personally directed to you. I doubt a proper English lady would reveal what went on in her bedroom to just anyone. Yet here she is giving you graphic detail."

"But you see that it's more than that. I am them. I'm seeing out of their eyes, tasting from their mouths, feeling from their skin. I now know what it's like for the kids. Being part of a greater whole as a twin as well as being yourself. It's helped me understand them in a way I don't think I ever could have before. A very strange side effect don't you think?"

"I do know you seem calmer with them when they get into 'twin' mode lately. Better able to make it work to your advantage. So I guess something good has come from all this. I just hate to see the stress it's put on you. I never know who's going to wake up, the sexy vixen? Or the frightened little girl? Not that I mind," he stresses. "I just know the toll it's taking on you."

"I'm ok, I have you to save me," she laughs as she gives him a bear hug.

Chapter 17

Wednesday
17 Oct '07

"Surprise Mommy!" The twins laughed as they climbed on the big four-poster bed, "We got you presents and daddy is having Cook make a fancy breakfast even though it isn't Sunday, all because it's your birthday." Their voices were so jumbled together it was hard to tell who was saying what.

"All right, calm yourselves please." She said while trying to gather them up in a big hug. Looking towards the doorway she saw Jackson standing there laughing.

"Well, you could help you know?" She laughed.

"And spoil all their fun? Would I do that Jeanette?" was his reply. He came into the room scooping up James, as Jeanette managed to grab onto Jasmine.

"You two need to let your mother finish waking up and get dressed if you want to have that fancy breakfast." Jack said to the children, in a fake stern voice.

"Yes, Sir!" they both replied together, trying not to laugh.

"Mummy when were you born?" asked Jasmine.

"You already know the answer to that," said James.

"But I like to hear Her say it! With all the numbers."

"OK, I'll say it," chuckled Jeanette, "With ALL the numbers: 11-11-77 at 11:11 am. Now the two of you go get dressed, and we'll meet you down stairs for breakfast."

Jack set down James as Jeanette let go of Jasmine and the kids ran from the room. With a wink and a smile, Jack closed the door after them and returned to the bed.

"May I help you with your nightclothes?" He asked, untying her gown as he kissed her.

Kissing, they fell back together. Slowly Jackson unbuttoned the gown that Jeanette wore, one button at a time, kissing the bared skin as he went. He usually hated these high-necked styles, but this was fun. Under the chin...on the throat...that cute little cleft where the collarbones meet...where her locket hangs...at the top of her cleavage... deep in the middle...at the bottom. This could take hours, as he leisurely drew circles along the edges of her breasts.

Jeanette let out a low moan. She had been trying to pretend indifference, being still, with a haughty look on her face. But a woman could only resist so much. Every nerve she had was tingling. She knew it wasn't "lady like," but she finally took his head and moved it to one exposed breast and said softly "Please!"

That's all he'd been waiting for; he lifted Jeanette up enough to remove her gown the rest of the way. "I want to see all of you," he murmured, caressing her body. "You keep getting more beautiful. More beautiful that when we first met. More beautiful than you were last year." He started kissing all those places he had been caressing, starting back at her breasts, and slowly circling to her navel, and then softly moving lower.

Walking down the stairs, Jeanette turned to Jackson and said, "I had the strangest dream last night. It was about one of those Colonial Natives. It was as if I were her, or something. I was seeing out of her eyes as her birthday celebration took place. It was very creepy. Then she died; she was run over by another savage on his horse. She said the oddest thing: "Beware 30...must warn the next."

114

"How very strange" replied Jack, "must have been all of Christopher's talking about his exploits during his visit."

"I would think so; it was certainly unsettling. I won't let it ruin the hunt, I did manage to block it out for a while there," she smiled at him, "yet it lingers."

The breakfast room was painted in creams and yellows to accent the east facing windows. Jeanette and Jackson were in full hunting regalia, carrying their hats.

Conversation during the meal centered on the Birthday hunt. Who would be here, who couldn't make it and why. Which children were likely to attend, and how far they would be allowed to ride with the Hunt. Who would be Nanny this year? If Uncle Milton would get thrown by his horse this year? Always a great topic for discussion.

After the dishes had been cleared and the tea had been refreshed, the children each picked up their presents and stood in front of their mother.

"Oh my, well who should go first?" Jeanette asked.

"I should, me! Me!" said James, jumping up and down. "I'm oldest!"

"BY only 5 minutes," replied Jasmine. "And you went first last year."

"Did Not!" whined James

"Yes you did, with that blue scarf you gave her. I remember!" Jasmine answered.

"Oh, yeah...then I guess it's your turn. Well hurry up. You're taking too long."

"Here mum, I made this all by my self. It's why I've been in my room reading so much lately."

"Why thank you Jasmine. What pretty paper, where did you find it?" Jeanette asked.

"Pappa took us into town with him last week when you went to see Aunt Susan. It was all a big surprise." Jasmine giggled. "Open it!"

Carefully, Jeanette opened the package and found a knitted bed jacket all done in light blues and greens, with a purple ribbon tie. "My! This is beautiful. Where did you learn to knit something this light and dainty? Not from me, that's for sure."

"It's actually crochet, and Sally taught me. It's really quite simple, once you have the right needle and the right thin yarns. That was the hard part. Trying to explain to Pappa what I needed when he went to town last month. But he did quite well," she said in a very grown up tone.

"Yes I can see that. And so did you! I'm very proud of you. This is so very soft. I can't wait to wear it tomorrow morning. Come here so I can give you a big hug." Jeanette moved her chair away from the table so she could embrace her daughter.

"My turn now!" said James as he pushed his present between his mother and sister. I made you something you really need. Not some silly old bed jacket. It's only a cape anyway."

"It's not silly; I worked very hard on that. And mum needs it to keep her shoulders warm in the mornings when she has her tea up stairs. Mum, tell him it's not silly!" whined Jasmine.

"James it's a very lovely bed jacket. The cape style lets me wear it over any of my gowns. Don't be bratty, or you shall spend the day in your room, and not with the others on the Hunt."

"I'm sorry, and I'm sorry to you too Jasmine…Will you open mine now Mummy?"

"Of course, let me put this down first." Jeanette placed the bed jacket on the table, and looked at the presents in her lap.

"The big one first, then the other one, they go together."

"That's fine, let's see what we have here…" Jasmine said as she opened the larger package. "…It's a? A? Let me take it out and get a good look at it."

"It a Jewelry holder. See, it's a hand, and you put it on its base like this." James took the smooth hand shaped piece of wood from his mother, and twisted it into the flat piece he removed from the wrappings. The hand stood up on the table.

"The fingers are curved so you can put your necklaces on them, and the thumb has wholes for your earrings. And this shallow place in the base is for your hair combs. It's walnut, from that branch that fell behind the stables. And I made it all myself."

"Well, isn't that inventive, who showed you how to do all that?" An amazed Jeanette inquired. She ran her hand over the wood, feeling how wonderfully smooth it was.

"Mickey, in the stables. He does a lot of wood stuff. He let me use his knives and files and everything. He showed me how to find the right piece of wood for what we was, I mean were making. How to make the base and the stand fit together, but still be able to come apart. This is for when you travel too. So you don't have to worry where everything gets to, it's all in one place. Isn't it super? Oh! Open the other one now!"

"All right James, calm yourself a bit, I'll open it now." Jeanette carefully opened the smaller package that was wrapped in tissue paper. *"Why, what a pretty Comb. Thank you James!"* she exclaimed as she pulled him into a hug. *"This will match the dress I'm wearing to the dance tonight. However did you know?"*

"Jasmine helped me on that one. She saw it when we all went to town. She knew I was looking for something to put on the tray. I thought this was pretty, and I had some money, 'cause my gift didn't really cost anything. I'm glad you like it."
"I really do. It's wonderful, as is the jewelry stand. I still can't believe the two of you are so grown up and so talented. Come here for another hug, both of you!"

"The guests are starting to arrive," Nancy announced, as she came in to finish tidying up the room, *"Mr. Groves has them by the gazebo as you requested. Your mounts are ready for you there as well."*

"Thank you Nancy," said Jeanette, "The children's presents took a while longer than we'd planned this morning. Could you please see that these other lovely gifts are taken to my room? I'll have to open them later."

Jeanette gave Nancy a smile over the twins' heads, so she'd let the other staff members know why their gifts hadn't been opened or acknowledged. It wouldn't do to slight anyone. They were the best help anywhere in the county, and she wouldn't want to lose them.

Over at the gazebo there were five riders with their horses so far, with others coming up the drive. They were expecting eight to ten families, with a few single friends and older relatives. A nice sized hunt, neither too big nor too small.

Peter, the groom, had Gentry and Queenie waiting, as well as, the two ponies. It was a lovely day for a hunt. The sun was shining, the birds were singing, there was a crisp feel to the air and the leaves crackled under the horse hooves. This was exactly what Jeanette had wished for in asking for good weather.

She loved the feel of Queenie, her horse, as she cantered across the fields. The strength of her, the feeling of freedom, like she could go anywhere, be anyone. Ahhh...if only that was possible, well for a few short minutes, it was, and she enjoyed it immensely.

The fox made a dash out of the trees and across a corner of the Peterson's cornfield with the hounds right behind, baying out their song. The hunters moved to canter as they came to open ground, enjoying the faster pace after all the time walking through the trees. It wasn't a large field, so they didn't get up much speed as they came to a large tree over a brook on the edge of an apple orchard. The fox was giving them quite a merry chase. Half of the hunters swerved off to the right, to go the long way around the orchard. The other half jumped the log and continued up the path through up middle after the dogs.

She was in the second group, the last to make the jump. Queenie was halfway over the log when the horse shied, throwing Jeanette off her back. Jeanette felt her leg snap when she hit the ground. She barely got a scream out, when Queenie fell back on her, crushing both legs and most of her lower body. She fainted. Queenie squirmed on the ground, then managed to stand on three legs.

Jackson heard Jeanette scream, whipped Gentry around, and was beside her in moments. He called to the others, who would come back as fast as they could, but just looking at her, he knew there was nothing anyone could do. Jeanette opened her eyes, smiled at Jack and whispered, "Beware 30...must warn the next!" She closed her eyes again and faded away.

"Not Jeanette too!" Jade yells as she awakens sobbing. "I can't take another death." Jake runs in from the shower, barely taking the time to wrap a towel around his sopping body in his hurry to get to her.

"I'm here baby," he murmurs, as he pulls her into his wet arms. "You're safe with me."

Jade sobs slowly diminish and she says, "Jeanette died, she was thrown from her horse in the hunt. Or, I guess it stumbled over a big tree and went down on top of her. It was all so real. I was her, I died, Again! I felt the pain, the fall to the ground, the breaking of her leg when she landed, the crushing when the horse fell back on her/me."

Jade gives a big shudder and buries her face in Jake's shoulder. As she finishes crying, Jade sits up and tries to explain what has scared her the most.

"She has my birth date," she says, "My exact birth date: 11-11-77 11:11am, and she said "Beware 30...must warn the next" too. What does it all mean? Am I losing it? This is all so scary. I don't know what to do."

"Well I do," states Jake, "we're both going to call in, and take a mental health day. We'll take a long drive and get you away from all this. How about we go to that restaurant you like up in Frederick for lunch."

119

Weakly she nods, "That sounds good. There's been so much lately, with one or the other of the Sisters sick, worrying about where we're being reassigned to, or if we even are. Maybe you're right; a mental health day sounds good. I'll call Alice on my cell, you go call in from my office, but grab a robe, the kids will be up soon."

The drive to Frederick is calming. Jake avoids the major expressways and takes a wandering route through Prince George, Montgomery and Frederick Counties. The leaves are in splendid color, the weather is warm enough to have the windows down if they keep their jackets mostly done up. The sun is shining, the birds are singing, you get the picture.

The Pesky PelyKan is a little known treasure on a side road near the county capital. The locals love it, most tourists can't find it, the food is great, the ambiance fun, and the prices are just perfect. Then there are the pelicans.

Jade loves pelicans. Their house has over a hundred of them in all shapes and sizes. The collection ranges from a 4-foot Capo de Monte' statue that Jake had picked up in Italy, to a ½ inch Schwartz crystal piece. They come in every conceivable color and material. From glass to wood to Buffalo tusk, and from life like to Picasso-isque. And that doesn't include the jewelry pieces.

Anything that she doesn't, have the PelyKan seems to. The owner's wife is just as big a fan as Jade. Most of what is on display is a lot larger than the family collection, but she loves to see what has been added, and talk about her favorite birds with the O'Hara's. It turns out to be a wonderful day after all.

Chapter 18

Thursday
18 Oct '07

"Liebhabering? Are you awake? Johanna?" Her husband whispered in her ear as she was slowly becoming conscious. "I'd like to give you your first birthday gift," he said with a twinkle in his voice.

"Not that again...Jarvis, you give me the same thing every year." She replied in mock annoyance, but couldn't stifle her laughter as he started to tickle her. Turning her gently, they'd just started to kiss when the door burst open, and 2 kids jumped on the bed.

"I told you she was awake." The little girl said, half-playful, half-bratty.

"But Vater said to wait until He opened the door," replied her brother, not really whining.

"Well I guess it's too late for that now. Come on kids, lets all kiss Mutter 30 times for her 30th Geburtstag!" So saying, they all tackled up on Johanna and kissed her everywhere they could manage. On her face, her neck, her arms, her hands, it became a wrestling match.

"Enough! Peace! I surrender! Let me up and I'll make you all some breakfast. You two go and get dressed, and we'll be down in a bit. Jan, be my big boy and put some more coals on the fires, but don't smother them. Joselyn, please get the table ready for breakfast. Ich Liber Dich Alles!"

The twins, scampered out of the room, closing the door as they went . Johanna turned back to her Jarvis. "Now about that present? I think you were about to unwrap it?"

"I think I can manage to find something to amuse you Schatzi, I know you like kisses here..." He said, trailing kisses up her arm towards her throat. "And here..." now kissing behind her ears, and nibbling on her ear lobes, "and here..." covering her mouth in a passionate kiss.

Jarvis was quite a kisser, each one even deeper than the last; it was as if he was trying to climb inside her heart, as it was melting into his. Both sets of hands were removing clothes, and caressing warm skin. Petting and playing, while the kisses continued to evolve into a total union of breaths and souls. Eventually the kisses started traveling to other body parts, after all everything tasted so good. And taste they did, from their nose to their toes, and various favorite spots in between.

Johanna cooked up wursts, and potato cakes. There was kaffe and milch for das kinder. Dark brot, and butter, fresh melone, and erdbeeres, in September! "Melons and strawberries, speak English! Johanna, coffee and milk, English!" she said aloud. "The children need the English!"

"And so do I, living in the big city of New York," she thought. "I need to speak better to do my shopping." The endless supply of foods delighted her in New York. She could find almost anything, all year round. "What a great city. To be sure, it had its problems, yet it was so good to us. Jarvis has a good job. The children go to a good school, right down the block. And the ease with which I can get all the shopping done, just great."

"Fruhstuck is ready!" She called. "I mean breakfast!"

As she walked into the dining room, Jarvis and the children shouted "Alles Gute Zum Geburtstag! Happy Birthday Muter!

Right where she had planned to place the platter of food were gaily-wrapped packages. Jarvis took the platter, "Here let me take that. You sit, and we'll serve you today." He said smiling, and placed the platter on the sideboard.

122

Jan pulled out her chair and Joselyn placed a ring of flowers in her hair as Johanna sat. "This is all lovely!" She said. "I wasn't expecting you to go to this much trouble."

"YOU only turn 30 once." Jarvis grinned. "You're old as me now."

"Only for 2 weeks Vater." Joselyn laughed, as Jan poured the Kaffe. "You'll be OLD again in 2 weeks"

"Thank you for that reminder kleiner madchen, I appreciate it." Jarvis picked up Joselyn and swung her around once, putting her right back in place.

"My turn," piped up Jan.

"I wouldn't forget you kleiner hosenmatz." Jarvis grabbed Jan and swung him harder, and plopped him down in his seat. "Time to eat before everything gets cold."

As they enjoyed the breakfast, Johanna said to Jarvis, "the dream I had night before...the Indian frau? This night I have a new one. The woman was in England. Was riche frau, a rich woman. Her 30 birthday also, she dies when they go on big fuchsjag, the foxhunting, for the rotfuchs. The pferd, the horse, she rides misses the big tree, and vom pferd fallen, she falls from the horse. The back, I think, it breaks, and more things. But she says the Beware 30...must warn the next! And she has my birth date. What does it mean Jarvis?"

"I have no knowing, it is very strange. We should talk more when the kinder are not here. They listen too well."

"This is true," replied Johanna, "Help me with the plates; I made applekuchen for a treat."

After the meal was cleaned up, Johanna asked to move the presents to the front room. She enjoyed sitting on the large sofa that backed to the big picture window overlooking the street.

How pretty the paper she had pasted on the walls, was in the morning light. The two large chairs by the fireplace were her mother's, the lace curtains his. A nice blend of the old world and this new one.

123

Sitting in the middle of the sofa, with one child on either side, Johanna said, "Now we are ready for the gifts!" and she started laughing.

"What is so funny muter?" asked Jan, "Why do you laugh?"

"The English, the word gift in English is to mean present. In German, the word pronounced like gift means poison. So I said it was time for poison. There are a few of the words like that; I cannot help but to laugh.

"I think I understand. Will you open whatever they are now?"

"Yes, I am ready; let's see what surprises my lovely family has for me."

"Jan may be first," said Joselyn.. "I went first last year."

"How do you remember?" asked Jan as he handed his mother a prettily wrapped box.

"I just do, I think it comes from being older," she laughed, "mostly from being a girl."

Johanna opened her gift to find a nice rectangular box with a carved lid. "My, how pretty, where did you get this?" She asked.

"I made it for you," answered Jan with pride. "Vater has been showing me how to carve the top. In school I took the class. I made the box. I hope you use it for your jewelry. I know you have some cloth to line it with. I just didn't know how to do it.

"I will do that. It is very lovely Jan, thank you so much. Come give me a kiss." Johanna hugged and kissed her son with much pride showing on her face.

"My turn!" smiled Joselyn, "I made my present also." She handed her mother a soft package, wrapped in paper, with many bows.

"Look at the pretty bows, Why so many of them?" asked Johanna laughing.

"There are five bows," answered Joselyn. *"2 kinder times 5 bows times the 10 years we are alive equals 30 years for you! I didn't have the ribbon for 30 bows, and the package is not that big. So I made a way to have a number that had a meaning."*

Jan just looked at her, "I would never have thought this. How do you do so well with the numbers? I think you will be in a bank when you grow up. You are just too fast with all the numbers."

"Numbers are just easy for me, you are the one who remembers all the dates and who did what in the history. I can never get them all straight. I think when we were made twins we each got half the brain." She laughed and the others joined in. "Now you can open the package Muter."

Johanna ripped the paper to find a lovely scarf and mittens. They were blue and green in a very pretty design. "Joselyn, did you crochet these by yourself? They are beautiful, and so warm."

"I do not have the hat finished. It is harder, because I wanted to make one that is fancy. I'm not so sure I will be able; I hope you will help me. I'm sorry I know you should not have to work on your own present. But it is very hard." Joselyn was almost in tears as she admitted this to her mother.

"Come here little one," cooed Johanna, "These are wonderful, I know the hats can be very hard. I would be very happy to help you. It is good for me to take the time to crochet as well. My fingers need the exercise." With hugs and kisses, she had Joselyn smiling in moments.

"So Johanna is confused," thinks Jade, "she should try being me! But she is me. This is all my imagination; I can't really be channeling spirits. David might believe in that sort of thing, but I don't think I really do. None of this is real, it can't be. How can I know these people, these women? How can this be happening? I don't talk to ghosts. Sure, I love that TV show, but let's be real. Yes, I know there are supposed to be people with those talents, but that ain't me! I don't have a drop of psychic blood in my body. If I did, wouldn't I have shown it before now? I mean I'm 30 for

125

Krimmney's sake...or damn near. Two weeks can't make that much difference. Arrrgh!"

"Okay, old girl," she said out loud. "Time to get up and at 'em. Always wondered who that 'em was, and did they know everyone was at them?" She started laughing at her silliness. That's how she coped with stress; making a joke out of it. If it was funny, it couldn't hurt you could it? You were safe as long as you were laughing right? She sure hoped so.

"Of course that's what all those people in the white coats thought too. Hmm, may have to rethink that just a little. Not right now, I better get moving if I want to take advantage of that shower I hear running."

After the shower, Jade tells Jake about Johanna's confusion at having the two dreams. And that she is having them two nights in a row, like Jade is.

Is this just her subconscious trying to make sense out of all this? Or is there some connection? The not knowing is driving her crazy. She wishes she could just ask the women what they want and get it over with. Then maybe the dreams would stop.

Chapter 19

Tuesday
23 Oct '07

She awoke slowly to the sounds of the little ones sleeping, knowing the sun was just beginning its rise. The arm around her slowly tightened as Black Hawk whispered, "Morning, my little Wolf, what do you wish on your birthing day?"

Smiling Lilac Wolf, turned to face her lover, her soul mate, her reason for being, and gently kissed him. "This is all I want. To be like this forever."

"That would spoil the kits' surprises, but if you wish…" and laughing, he rolled to her and started her morning with the softest kiss. Slowly it grew stronger, as his hands lightly caressed her ear lobes and teased her neck. Trailing kisses across her chin, he began nibbling on the sensitive lobe, and licking that lovely spot right behind it.

Lilac Wolf stretched her body so it was better lined up with his, and gave a bit of a purr. Gently she ran her hand in circles on her Hawk's outer thigh. Softly enough to tickle… not that a great warrior could be tickled of course! As he started kissing down her throat, she started caressing up his thigh.

Hawk was kissing lower and lower, she was circling higher and higher. Both were trying to keep their moans of pleasure quiet so the kits stayed asleep. Just as she reached that sensitive crease between leg and body,

he took her nipple in his mouth. She gasped with pleasure, her whole body on fire.

After a moment of pure ecstasy, her mind cleared enough to take him in her hand and run her fingers up and down the firm thickness of him. It was her turn to make him gasp. A few well-placed caresses along the top of his magnificent manhood had him more than ready to finish pleasing her. And please her he did!

They had barely finished when both kits were on top of them. "The sun rises, your day is here!" the little ones exclaimed. "Are you going to stay in the furs for ever? We can see the light."

"Now Turq, you know I get this one day, to enjoy the furs until the sun is over the river. Would you have me spoil the surprise of your aunts, as they make my birthing day meal?"

"It's not our sire's day, why does he stay in the furs?" asked Grey pup.

"It's my job to keep her warm," answered Black Hawk, with a smile for the boy, and a wink for Lilac Wolf. "It wouldn't do for her to catch a chill on this day would it?" he asked, trying to look serious.

"I guess not." Said the pup, with his head hung down, "I wouldn't like that."

"I wouldn't either," piped up Turquoise chick.

"Why so glum little pup?" asked Lilac Wolf.

"I can't give you your birth gift in the hut. Now I have to wait for the sun, and it moves so slowly." He said.

With that, Black Hawk picked him up and carried him out of their home.

"And you? You're being rather quiet little chick."

"I can wait; my gift can be given any time." Turq said with a smile. She helped her mother dress in her best leggings; braid her hair, put on her necklaces of shells and beads. Drape a raccoon skin cape over her

shoulders, and don her moccasins. Then they shook out the furs, and stacked them away, setting the hut in order for the day.

Mother and daughter left the hut and walked towards the central fire, hand in hand. Others were gathering, everyone called greetings to Lilac Wolf and Turquoise chick. It was a happy, loving, family feeling that enveloped the scene in an early morning mist. The fire was blazing with many cook pots around it. Blankets and furs had been spread around the sunny end of the clearing. All the children were running and playing as if this was a holiday.

Thirty summers, thought Lilac Wolf, where did it all go? I feel as young as Turquoise and Grey, yet I'm to be entering the elder woman's counsel this night. I start my year of trial. Am I ready? Can I really lead the women? Can I stand up to the men? I don't feel all that wise today. Will I be in only 1 year? It seems so long and yet so short. How is this possible? Why have I been so blessed?

Lilac Wolf looked around her. They were a small village of Catawba, only seven hands of huts, in rough circles on the west edge of the Iswa river. The long house facing the water and the morning sun with the ceremonial fire in the clearing before it. The sweat lodge was to the north, and the woman's lodge way off to the south. All surrounded by young tree trunks dug into the earth to form a barrier. One opening was easier to defend, from their enemies and from the bears that liked to raid their camp. Small fields now lay fallow, just past the edge of the village; the sun was shining on the water, as it slowly passed the horizon.

She said a silent prayer of thanks to "He who Never Dies", then joined her family for the celebration. She was led to a place of honor and seated on a large bearskin. Her sister brought her a bowl of apples and nuts to start the meal. An aunt served a mash of squash and corn with honey in it, and some roasted rabbit from this morning's kill. The tea like beverage of herbs was warm and spicy as Turquoise chick handed her a small cup.

Once she was served, everyone else went to the pots to get their food. The Braves ate first, or at least were served first. Then came the boys, next were the mothers, with the maidens and little girls, last in line. Today the order made no real difference, there was plenty of food for all, but in the dead of winter, it could be crucial. Everyone sat around and

129

talked as they ate. The dogs wandered around looking for handouts, children slipped them bites when they thought no one was looking, and the adults ignored it, in the spirit of celebration.

When the eating was finished, Great Eagle, the Medicine Man, stood to begin the blessings of the day. He'd barely started when the sentries shouted alarm, "The Cherokee Come!"

Everyone scattered screaming, mothers grabbing children, running for their huts. Warriors were looking for their bows and running for their horses. The enemy was upon them before Lilac Wolf's people could protect themselves. She had almost gotten into her hut, had just pushed the children to safety, when a Cherokee Brave rode right over her. The horse knocked her on her back, and stepped on her chest with his fourth leg. The Brave never saw Lilac Wolf. It only took a moment.

Lilac Wolf got half a scream out. Once the horse was past, the kits ran to her crying, "Don't die, don't die!" Turq cradled her head, as Grey held her hand sobbing. Black Hawk was there as if by magic.

She looked up at them and murmured "Beware 30...must warn next!" And faded away.

"Are you alright Jade?" asked Alicia, "You seem rather down this morning. Not your usual chipper self."

"I just haven't been sleeping well lately. I've been having these strange dreams. I can't seem to get rid of them. They are driving me nuts."
"Well, have you tried talking to someone about them?"

"Sure, I've told Jake all about them, and it hasn't helped much."

"I meant a friend or a professional. I know you've been under a lot of stress since you found out that you may be moving overseas this spring."

"I know what you mean, but they started a whole month before we even found out about the move. They seem to be centered on my turning 30. You know that I've never been bothered by my age.

130

I'm not one of those women who care that I'm getting older, or that I'm not a size 4 anymore, not that I'd complain if I could see a size 6 once in a while. I just don't know what's going on in my head."

"Alice and I are here if you need someone to talk to dear, you know that. Just say the word and we'll close the shop and go out for cappuccinos and a good long chat."

"Thanks Alicia, I really appreciate it. I may take you up on that if this gets any crazier," said Jade, "but for now, I have to get the Andersons booked to Disney over spring break, and see if I can get any last minute air to London for Thanksgiving weekend. But thanks again, it really means a lot."

"Any time dear," was Alicia's response as she returned to the office, "any time."

Chapter 20

Wednesday
24 Oct '07

"Surprise Mommy!" The twins laughed as they climbed on the big four-poster bed, "We got you presents and daddy is having Cook make a fancy breakfast even though it isn't Sunday, all because it's your birthday." Their voices were so jumbled together it was hard to tell who was saying what.

"All right, calm yourselves please." She said while trying to gather them up in a big hug. Looking towards the doorway she saw Jackson standing there laughing.

"Well, you could help you know?" She laughed.

"And spoil all their fun? Would I do that Jeanette?" was his reply. He came into the room scooping up James, as Jeanette managed to grab onto Jasmine.

"You two need to let your mother finish waking up and get dressed if you want to have that fancy breakfast." Jack said to the children, in a fake stern voice.

"Yes, Sir!" they both replied together, trying not to laugh.

"Mummy when were you born?" asked Jasmine.

"You already know the answer to that," said James.

"But I like to hear Her say it! With all the numbers."

"OK, I'll say it," chuckled Jeanette, "With ALL the numbers: 11-11-77 at 11:11 am. Now the two of you go get dressed, and we'll meet you down stairs for breakfast."

Jack set down James as Jeanette let go of Jasmine and the kids ran from the room. With a wink and a smile, Jack closed the door after them and returned to the bed.

"May I help you with your nightclothes?" He asked, untying her gown as he kissed her.

Kissing, they fell back together. Slowly Jackson unbuttoned the gown that Jeanette wore, one button at a time, kissing the bared skin as he went. He usually hated these high-necked styles, but this was fun. Under the chin...on the throat...that cute little cleft where the collarbones meet...where her locket hangs...at the top of her cleavage...deep in the middle...at the bottom. This could take hours, as he leisurely drew circles along the edges of her breasts.

Jeanette let out a low moan. She had been trying to pretend indifference, being still, with a haughty look on her face. But a woman could only resist so much. Every nerve she had was tingling. She knew it wasn't "Lady" like, but she finally took his head and moved it to one exposed breast and said softly "Please!"

That's all he'd been waiting for; he lifted Jeanette up enough to remove her gown the rest of the way. "I want to see all of you," he murmured, caressing her body. "You keep getting more beautiful. More beautiful that when we first met. More beautiful than you were last year." He started kissing all those places he had been caressing, starting back at her breasts, and slowly circling to her navel, and then softly moving lower.

Walking down the stairs, Jeanette turned to Jackson and said, "I had the strangest dream last night. It was about one of those Colonial Natives. It was as if I were her, or something. I was seeing out of her eyes as her birthday celebration took place. It was very creepy. Then she died; she was run over by another savage on his horse. She said the oddest thing: "Beware 30...must warn the next."

134

"How very strange" replied Jack, "must have been all of Christopher's talking about his exploits during his visit."

"I would think so; it was certainly unsettling. I won't let it ruin the hunt, I did manage to block it out for a while there," she smiled as him, "yet it lingers."

The breakfast room was done up in creams and yellows to accent the east facing windows. Jeanette and Jackson were in full hunting regalia, carrying their hats.

Conversation during the meal centered on the Birthday hunt. Who would be here, who couldn't make it and why. Which children were likely to attend, and how far they would be allowed to ride with the Hunt. Who would be Nanny this year? If Uncle Milton would get thrown by his horse this year? Always a great topic for debate.

After the dishes had been cleared and the tea had been refreshed, the children each picked up their presents and stood in front of their mother.

"Oh my, well who should go first?" Jeanette asked.

"I should, me! Me!" said James, jumping up and down. "I'm oldest!"

"BY only 5 minutes," replied Jasmine. "And you went first last year."

"Did Not!" whined James

"Yes you did, with that blue scarf you gave her. I remember!" Jasmine's answered.

"Oh, yeah...then I guess it's your turn. Well hurry up. You're taking too long."

"Here mum, I made this all by my self. It's why I've been in my room reading so much lately."

"Why thank you Jasmine. What pretty paper, where did you find it?" Jeanette asked.

"Pappa took us into town with him last week when you went to see Aunt Susan. It was all a big surprise." Jasmine giggled. *"Open it!"*

Carefully, Jeanette opened the package and found a knitted bed jacket all done in light blues and greens, with a purple ribbon tie. *"My! This is beautiful. Where did you learn to knit something this light and dainty? Not from me, that's for sure."*

"It's actually crochet, and Sally taught me. It's really quite simple, once you have the right needle and the right thin yarns. That was the hard part. Trying to explain to Pappa what I needed when he went to town last month. But he did quite well," she said in a very grown up tone.

"Yes I can see that, so did you! I'm very proud of you. This is so very soft. I can't wait to wear it tomorrow morning. Come here so I can give you a big hug." And so saying, Jeanette moved her chair away from the table so she could embrace her daughter.

"My turn now!" James said as he pushed his present between his mother and sister. *I made you something you really need. Not some silly old bed jacket. It's only a cape anyway."*

"It's not silly; I worked very hard on that. And mum needs it to keep her shoulders warm in the mornings when she has her tea up stairs. Mum, tell him it's not silly!" whined Jasmine.

"James it's a very lovely bed jacket. The cape style lets me wear it over any of my gowns. Don't be bratty, or you shall spend the day in your room, and not with the others on the Hunt."

"I'm sorry, and I'm sorry to you too Jasmine…Will you open mine now Mummy?"

"Of course, let me put this down first." Jeanette placed the bed jacket on the table, and looked at the presents in her lap.

"The big one first, then the other one, they go together."

"That's fine, let's see what we have here…" Jasmine said as she opened the larger package. "…It's a? A? Let me take it out and get a good look at it."

"It a Jewelry holder. See, it's a hand, and you put it on its base like this." James took the smooth hand shaped piece of wood from his mother, and twisted it into the flat piece he removed from the wrappings. The hand stood up on the table.

"The fingers are curved so you can put your necklaces on them, and the thumb has wholes for your earrings. And this shallow place in the base is for your hair combs. It's walnut, from that branch that fell behind the stables. And I made it all myself."

"Well, isn't that inventive, who showed you how to do all that?" An amazed Jeanette inquired. She ran her hand over the wood, feeling how wonderfully smooth it was.

"Mickey, in the stables. He does a lot of wood stuff. He let me use his knives and files and everything. He showed me how to find the right piece of wood for what we was, I mean were making. And how to make the base and the stand fit together, but still be able to come apart. This is for when you travel too. So you don't have to worry where everything gets to, it's all in one place. Isn't it super? Oh! Open the other one now!"

"All right James, calm yourself a bit, I'll open it now." Jeanette carefully opened the smaller package that was wrapped in tissue paper. "Why, what a pretty Comb. Thank you James!" she exclaimed as she pulled him into a hug. "This will match the dress I'm wearing to the dance tonight. However did you know?"

"Jasmine helped me on that one. She saw it when we all went to town. She knew I was looking for something to put on the tray. I thought this was pretty, and I had some money, 'cause my gift didn't really cost anything. I'm glad you like it."

"I really do. It's wonderful, as is the jewelry stand. I still can't believe the two of you are so grown up and so talented. Come here for another hug, both of you!"

"The guests are starting to arrive," Nancy announced, as she came in to finish tidying up the room, "Mr. Groves has them by the gazebo as you requested. Your mounts are ready for you there as well."

"Thank you Nancy," said Jeanette, "The children's presents took a while longer than we'd planned this morning. Could you please see that these other lovely gifts are taken to my room? I'll have to open them later."

Jeanette gave Nancy a smile over the twin's heads, so she'd let the other staff members know why their gifts hadn't been opened or acknowledged. It wouldn't do to slight anyone. They were the best help anywhere in the county, and she wouldn't want to lose them.

Over at the gazebo there were five riders with their horses so far, with others coming up the drive. They were expecting eight to ten families, with a few single friends and older relatives. A nice sized hunt, neither too big nor too small.

Peter, the groom, had Gentry and Queenie waiting, as well as, the two ponies. It was a lovely day for a hunt. The sun was shining, the birds were singing, there was a crisp feel to the air and the leaves crackled under the horse hooves. This was exactly what Jeanette had wished for in asking for good weather. She loved the feel of Queenie, her horse, as she cantered across the fields. The strength of her, the feeling of freedom, like she could go anywhere, be anyone. Ahhh...if only that was possible, well for a few short minutes, it was, and she enjoyed it immensely.

The fox made a dash out of the trees and across a corner of the Peterson's cornfield with the hounds right behind, baying out their song. The hunters moved to canter as they came to open ground, enjoying the faster pace after all the time walking through the trees. It wasn't a large field, so they didn't get up much speed as they came to a large tree over a brook on the edge of an apple orchard. The fox was giving them quite a merry chase. Half of the hunters swerved off to the right, to go the long way around the orchard. The other half jumped the log and continued up the path through up middle after the dogs.

She was in the second group, the last to make the jump. Queenie was halfway over the log when the horse shied throwing Jeanette off her back. Jeanette felt her leg snap when she hit the ground. She barely got a scream out, when Queenie fell back on her, crushing both legs and most of her lower half. She fainted. Queenie squirmed on the ground, then managed to stand.

Jackson heard Jeanette scream, whipped Gentry around, and was beside her in moments. He called to the others, who would come back as fast as they could, but just looking at her, he knew there was nothing anyone could do. Jeanette opened her eyes, smiled at Jack and whispered, "Beware 30...must warn the next!" She closed her eyes again and faded away.

"This is damn unbelievable." Jade wakes up talking to herself. Not that this is anything new anymore. It has been so long since she's waken up without either having had one of the dreams, or being afraid that she'll have one of the dreams. She seems to be always waking up in a state of agitation.

She can't remember the quiet, peaceful mornings, when she would lie in bed and let the morning wash over her. She loved getting up to her leisurely shower, taking her time dressing, playing with her hair and makeup, simply enjoying her self in the morning. Where had it all gone? Why is this happening? And when will it ever stop?

Getting up she looks around her room at the geometric quilt in bold blues and greens. At the strong photos on her walls, all very stark, each a close-up study of an object in nature, from a seashell to a leaf to a grasshopper. They are all framed in simple white frames, and placed in no obvious fashion along the two sidewalls of the room. Some are in color, others in black and white. She's even managed sepia for a few of them. Jade is still learning the developing side of photography. Her whole house tends to be the display area for her work.

She hasn't decided if she liked taking the pictures, or developing them the best yet. That is the frustrating point in all this dream business. It just doesn't develop into a clear picture for her. If this was one of her negatives, she'd toss it out as damaged, impossible to repair. But how do you do that to a dream?

139

She's tried writing everything down, tracking it to make some sense of it. But other than which woman on which day, she can't see a pattern, besides the repeated warnings. Just a bad negative that made a very fuzzy photo.

Chapter 21

Thursday
25 Oct '07

"Liebhabering? Are you awake? Johanna?" Her husband whispered in her ear as she was slowly becoming conscious. "I'd like to give you your first birthday gift," he said with a twinkle in his voice.

"Not that again...Jarvis, you give me the same thing every year." She replied in mock annoyance, but couldn't stifle her laughter as he started to tickle her. Turning her gently, they'd just started to kiss when the door burst open, and 2 kids jumped on the bed.

"I told you she was awake." The little girl said, half-playful, half-bratty.

"But Vater said to wait until HE opened the door," replied her brother, not really whining.

"Well I guess it's too late for that now. Come on kids, lets all kiss Mutter 30 times for her 30th Geburtstag!" So saying, they all ganged up on Johanna and kissed her everywhere they could manage. On her face, her neck, her arms, her hands, it became a wrestling match.

"Enough! Peace! I surrender! Let me up and I'll make you all some breakfast. You two go and get dressed, and we'll be down in a bit. Jan, be my big boy and put some more coals on the fires, but don't smother them. Joselyn, please get the table ready for breakfast. Ich Liber Dich Alles!"

The twins scampered out of the room, closing the door as they went . Johanna turned back to her Jarvis. "Now about that present? I think you were about to unwrap it?"

Jarvis came back to the bed and climbed back under the covers.

"I think I can manage to find something to amuse you Schatzi, I know you like kisses here..." He said, trailing kisses up her arm towards her throat. "And here..." now kissing behind her ears, and nibbling on her ear lobes, "and here..." covering her mouth in a passionate kiss.

Jarvis was quite a kisser, each one even deeper than the last; it was as if he was trying to climb inside her heart, as it was melting into his. Both sets of hands were removing clothes, and caressing warm skin. Petting and playing, while the kisses continued to evolve into a total union of breaths and souls. Eventually the kisses started traveling to other body parts, after all everything tasted so good. And taste they did, from their nose to their toes, and various favorite spots in between.

Johanna cooked up wursts, and potato cakes. There was kaffe and milch for das kinder. Dark brot, and butter, fresh melone, and erdbeeres, in September! "Melons and strawberries, speak English! Johanna, coffee and milk, English!" she said aloud. "The children need the English!"

"And so do I, living in the big city of New York," she thought. "I need to speak better to do my shopping." The endless supply of foods delighted her in New York. She could find almost anything, all year round. "What a great city. To be sure, it had its problems, yet it was so good to us. Jarvis has a good job. The children go to a good school, right down the block. And the ease with which I can get all the shopping done, just great."

"Fruhstuck is ready!" She called. "I mean breakfast!"

As she walked into the dining room, Jarvis and the children shouted "Alles Gute Zum Geburtstag! Happy Birthday Muter!

Right where she had planned to place the platter of food were gaily-wrapped packages. Jarvis took the platter, "Here let me take that. You

142

sit, and we'll serve you today." He said smiling, and placed the platter on the sideboard.

Jan pulled out her chair and Joselyn placed a ring of flowers in her hair as Johanna sat. "This is all lovely!" She said. "I wasn't expecting you to go to this much trouble."

"YOU only turn 30 once." Jarvis grinned. "You're old as me now."

"Only for 2 weeks Vater." Joselyn laughed, as Jan poured the Kaffe. "You'll be OLD again in 2 weeks"

"Thank you for that reminder kleiner madchen, I appreciate it." Jarvis picked up Joselyn and swung her around once, putting her right back in place.

"My turn," piped up Jan.

"I wouldn't forget you kleiner hosenmatz." Jarvis grabbed Jan and swung him harder, and plopped him down in his seat. "Time to eat before everything gets cold."

As they enjoyed the breakfast, Johanna said to Jarvis, "the dream I had night before...the Indian frau? This night I have a new one. The woman was in England. Was riche frau, a rich woman. Her 30 birthday also, she dies when they go on big Fuchsjagd. The foxhunting, for the rotfuchs. The pferd, the horse, she rides misses the big tree, and vom pferd fallen, she falls from the horse. The back, I think, it breaks, and more things. But she says the Beware 30...must warn the next! She had my birth date. What does it mean Jarvis?"

"I have no knowing, it is very strange. We should talk more when the kinder are not here. They listen too well."

"This is true," replied Johanna, "Help me with the plates; I made applekuchen for a treat."

After the meal was cleaned up, Johanna asked to move the presents to the front room. She enjoyed sitting on the large sofa that backed to the big picture window overlooking the street.

143

How pretty the paper she had pasted on the walls was in the morning light. The two large chairs by the fireplace were her mother's, the lace curtains his. A nice blend of the old world and this new one.

Sitting in the middle of the sofa, with one child on either side, Johanna said, "Now we are ready for the gifts!" and she started laughing.

"What is so funny muter?" asked Jan, "Why do you laugh?"

"The English, the word gift in English is to mean present. But in German, the word pronounced like gift means poison. So I said it was time for poison. There are a few of the words like that; I cannot help but to laugh.

"I think I understand. Will you open whatever they are now?"

"Yes, I am ready now; let's see what surprises my lovely family has for me."

"Jan may be first," said Joselyn. "I went first last year."

"How do you remember?" asked Jan as he handed his mother a prettily wrapped box.

"I just do, I think it comes from being older," she laughed, "mostly from being a girl."

Johanna opened her gift to find a nice rectangular box with a carved lid. "My, how pretty, where did you get this?" She asked.

"I made it for you," answered Jan with pride. "Vater has been showing me how to carve the top. In school I took the class. I made the box. I hope you use it for your jewelry. I know you have some cloth to line it with. I just didn't know how to do it.

"I will do that. It is very lovely Jan, thank you so much. Come give me a kiss." Johanna hugged and kissed her son with much pride showing on her face.

"My turn!" smiled Joselyn, "I made my present also." She handed her mother a soft package, wrapped in paper, with many bows.

144

"Look at the pretty bows, Why so many of them?" asked Johanna laughing.

"There are five bows," answered Joselyn. "2 kinder times 5 bows times the 10 years we are alive equals 30 years for you! I didn't have the ribbon for 30 bows, and the package is not that big. So I made a way to have a number that had a meaning."

Jan just looked at her, "I would never have thought this. How do you do so well with the numbers? I think you will be in a bank when you grow up. You are just too fast with all the numbers."

"Numbers are just easy for me, you are the one who remembers all the dates and who did what in the history. I can never get them all straight. I think when we were made twins we each got half the brain." She laughed and the others joined in. "Now you can open the package Muter."

Johanna ripped the paper to find a lovely scarf and mittens. They were blue and green in a very pretty design. "Joselyn, did you crochet these by yourself? They are beautiful, and so warm."

"I do not have the hat finished. It is harder, because I wanted to make one that is fancy. I'm not so sure I will be able; I hope you will help me. I'm sorry I know you should not have to work on your own present. But it is very hard." Joselyn was almost in tears as she admitted this to her mother.

"Come here little one," cooed Johanna, "These are wonderful, I know the hats can be very hard. I would be very happy to help you. It is good for me to take the time to crochet as well. My fingers need the exercise." With hugs and kisses, she had Joselyn smiling in moments.

"And now for my present," said Jarvis. "We must go to the store to see it. It could not be ready until this morning."

"What is it Vater?" asked Jan. "Will you tell us, and only make Muter wait?"

"No," Jarvis said. "It will be a surprise for everyone. Let's get the coats, Johanna you can use your new scarf and mittens. It is very cold today, and the snow is to fall. But we only walk a few streets."

Everyone bundled up and set off to the mystery store for Johanna's present. It turned out to be to a jewelry store that Jarvis led them. "What is this?" asked Johanna, "I don't need any jewelry."

"Come," he said, leading the way into the store. "I'm here to pick up my purchase." Jarvis told the clerk behind the counter, handing him a slip of paper.

Reading it the clerk replied, "I have it right here Mr. Waggoner, did you want it gift wrapped?"

"No, I would like her to wear it home please," he answered. The clerk brought over a small box and handed it to Jarvis. Opening it towards Johanna, he got down on one knee and said, "I could not offer you the engagement ring when we wed, and for these 13 years, all you have is your wedding band. Now I am giving you the engagement ring, so I ask again 'Will you marry me?"

Johanna was overwhelmed with emotions. The simple gold band with 1/3-carat solitaire diamond was beautiful, more beautiful than anything she had ever seen. However, her big strong husband, on his knee, in the store was just too much. She began to cry as she said, "Ja, I will marry you, again and again and again! I love you, you wonderful man; now get up before you hurt yourself. You are embarrassing me."

Jarvis stood and put the ring on Johanna's finger then gave her the biggest hug in the world. The grin on his face went from ear to ear, and threatened to split it in two. How he could be so happy he'd never understand, he just knew it all came from his Johanna.

The kinder were clamoring around to see the ring. As they were getting a bit rowdy, the family moved out to the street. Enjoying the way the diamond shone in the sunlight, Johanna smiled even brighter. "We should be getting home," she said. "The kinder still have to go to the school after the lunch. And even if it is my birthday, the cleaning must be done." The happy family started their three-block walk home.

146

When they were crossing the first intersection, a carriage came racing around the corner. The horse looked frightened, its eyes wide and not seeing anything. The driver of the carriage was calling for the horse to stop, and yelling for people to move out of the way. Jarvis and Jan were most of the way across and out of danger, but Joselyn and Johanna were in the middle of the street.

As Johanna yelled to run, Joselyn froze in terror, staring at the horse running right at her. Johanna moved to her daughter and shoved her aside, just as the horse came upon her. There was no chance for Johanna to save herself. The horse knocked her down and continued right over her. Only two of the carriage wheels hit her, but it was enough. As Jarvis and the children ran back to her, she looked up at them and said, 'Beware 30...must warn the next!" She died in their arms.

"Johanna!" yells Jade as she springs from her bed, half-asleep, and totally crazed. "Not you too! Why? Why you too? I don't understand any of this."

Jake comes in from the bathroom, by now all too used to the morning commotions. He puts his arms around Jade as she wakes fully, and murmurs soothing things in her ear. Once she has calmed down slightly he asks her about this latest dream. Jade explains about the lovely family scene with the presents, and the trip to the store to pick up the one from Jarvis. She tells him about the carriage, how Johanna had saved Joselyn, and was then killed. Saying, "Beware 30...must warn the next!" before she died. And that she has the same birth date too.

Jake lets her talk herself out, until she is simply sobbing into his shoulder. Once she stops, he suggests Jade call in and take the morning off. She's only working a half-day today anyway. Maybe she should start the family's Christmas shopping. A day of Retail Therapy will probably take her mind off all this dream stuff.

Feeling more like herself, Jade takes a few seconds to think this over, and agrees. There's nothing pending at work and a day spent shopping will be very therapeutic. She gives Jake a very big kiss, and goes off to shower and get dressed.

When she calls Alice, she is not only given the green light, but asked to pick up a specific present for Alicia. "So much for the boss being mad about you taking time off." She thinks.

The mall is just what she needs. The throngs of people, the noise of music and voices, the general hustle and bustle, has her in a good mood within minutes of arrival. Jade manages to find Alice's gift to Alicia first thing. For her mother she locates a wonderful room divider that has places on all six sides to put three different 8" X 10" pictures. She can place some photos of the children, as well as a few pieces of their school artwork. This still left plenty of room for prints from other family members, and she knows just where it will fit.

Then there are quite a few odds and ends for the kids and a few things for her. Over four hours at the big mall would change anyone's mood. While most people become grumpy and slightly crazed, Jade becomes energized and happy. Give her Retail Therapy any day.

Chapter 22

Tuesday
30 Oct '07

She awoke slowly to the sounds of the little ones sleeping, knowing the sun was just beginning its rise. The arm around her slowly tightened as Black Hawk whispered, "Morning, my little Wolf, what do you wish on your birthing day?"

Smiling Lilac Wolf turned to face her lover, her soul mate, her reason for being, and gently kissed him. "This is all I want. To be like this forever."

"That would spoil the kits' surprises, but if you wish…" and laughing, he rolled to her and started her morning with the softest kiss. Slowly it grew stronger, as his hands lightly caressed her ear lobes and teased her neck. Trailing kisses across her chin, he began nibbling on the sensitive lobe, and licking that lovely spot right behind it.

Lilac Wolf stretched her body so it was better lined up with his, and gave a bit of a purr. Slowly she ran her hand in circles on her Hawk's outer thigh. Softly enough to tickle… not that a great warrior could be tickled of course! As he started kissing down her throat, she started caressing up his thigh.

Hawk was kissing lower and lower, she was circling higher and higher. Both were trying to keep their moans of pleasure quiet, so the kits stayed asleep. Just as she reached that sensitive crease between leg and body,

149

he took her nipple in his mouth. She gasped with pleasure, her whole body on fire.

After a moment of pure ecstasy, her mind cleared enough to take him in her hand and run her fingers up and down the firm thickness of him. It was her turn to make him gasp. A few well-placed caresses along the top of his magnificent manhood had him more than ready to finish pleasing her. And please her he did!

They had barely finished when both kits were on top of them "The sun rises, your day is here!" The little ones exclaimed. "Are you going to stay in the furs for ever? We can see the light."

"Now Turq, you know I get this one day, to enjoy the furs until the sun is over the river's edge. Would you have me spoil the surprise of your aunts, as they make my birth morning meal?"

"It's not our sire's day, why does he stay in the furs?" asked Grey pup.

"It's my job to keep her warm," answered Black Hawk, with a smile for the boy, and a wink for Lilac Wolf. "It wouldn't do for her to catch a chill on this day would it?" he asked, trying to look serious.

"I guess not," said the pup, with his head hung down," I wouldn't like that."

"I wouldn't either," piped up Turquoise chick.

"Why so glum little pup?" asked Lilac Wolf.

"I can't give you your birth gift in the tepee. Now I have to wait for the sun, and it moves so slowly," he pouted.

Black Hawk stepped into his leggings and moccasins, picked up Grey pup and carried him out of the hut.
"And you? You're being rather quiet my little chick."

"I can wait; my gift can be given any time." Turq said with a smile. She helped her mother dress in her best buckskin tunic and leggings; braid feathers into her hair; put on her necklaces of shells and beads; slip on her moccasins; and drape a raccoon skin cape over her shoulder. Then

they shook out the furs, and stacked them away, setting the hut in order for the day.

Mother and daughter left the hut and walked towards the central fire, hand in hand. Others were gathering, everyone called greetings to Lilac Wolf and Turquoise chick. It was a happy, loving, family feeling that enveloped the scene in an early morning mist. The fire was blazing with many cook pots around it. Blankets and furs had been spread around the sunny end of the clearing. All the children were running and playing as if this was a holiday.

Thirty summers, thought Lilac Wolf, where did it all go? I feel as young as Turquoise and Grey, yet I'm to be entering the elder woman's counsel this night. I start my year of trial. Am I ready? Can I really lead the women? Can I stand up to the men? I don't feel all that wise today. Will I be in only 1 year? It seems so long and yet so short. How is this possible? Why have I been so blessed?

Lilac Wolf looked around her. They were a small village of Catawba, only seven hands of huts, in rough circles on the west edge of the Iswa river. The long house facing the water and the morning sun with the ceremonial fire in the clearing before it. The sweat lodge was to the north, and the woman's lodge way off to the south. All surrounded by young tree trunks dug into the earth to form a barrier. One opening was easier to defend, from their enemies and from the bears that liked to raid their camp. Small fields now lay fallow, just past the edge of the village; the sun was shining on the water, as it slowly passed the horizon.

She said a silent prayer of thanks to "He who Never Dies", then joined her family for the celebration. She was led to a place of honor and seated on a large bearskin. Her sister brought her a bowl of apples and nuts to start the meal. An aunt served a mash of squash and corn with honey in it, and some roasted rabbit from this morning's kill. The tea like beverage of herbs was warm and spicy as Turquoise chick handed her a small cup.

Once she was served, everyone else went to the pots to get their food. The Braves ate first, or at least were served first. Then came the boys, next were the mothers, with the maidens and little girls, last in line. Today the order made no real difference, there was plenty of food for all, but in the dead of winter, it could be crucial. Everyone sat around and

151

talked as they ate. The dogs wandered around looking for handouts, children slipped them bites when they thought no one was looking, and the adults ignored it, in the spirit of celebration.

When the eating was finished, Great Eagle, the Medicine Man, stood to begin the blessings of the day. He'd barely started when the sentries shouted alarm, "The Cherokee Come!"

Everyone scattered screaming, mothers grabbing children, running for their huts. Warriors were looking for their bows and running for their horses. The enemy was upon them before Lilac Wolf's people could protect themselves. She had almost gotten into her hut, had just pushed the children to safety, when a Cherokee Brave rode right over her. The horse knocked her on her back, and stepped on her chest with his hind leg. The Brave never saw Lilac Wolf; it was over in a moment.

Lilac Wolf got half a scream out. Once the horse was past, the kits ran to her crying, "Don't die, don't die!" Turq cradled her head, as Grey held her hand sobbing. Black Hawk was there as if by magic.

She looked up at them and murmured "Beware 30…must warn next!" And faded away.

Even though Jade "was" Lilac Wolf in the dream, she feels as if the Indian woman has been staring into her eyes when she dies, not at her families. This message is meant for her, she is the one who has to beware. "But why? She isn't going to be run down by some raiding Indian. She is safe and happy, so why all this warning? Should she really be worried?" She wished she knew.

"Once again, Jake is at a morning meeting when I need him. But then I always need him lately. It's a wonder the guy doesn't go running screaming in the opposite direction every time he sees me. Well, the sex is good, OK, GREAT! But a man can't live on that alone. He needs some psychic stability here at home, with everything going on at work. And I don't think I'm providing a lot of that these days.

Maybe I'll do something special for him tonight. Make him a nice dinner. With the grocery shopping I did yesterday, I have everything I need to prepare something more than burgers or mac and cheese. Now what should I make? We haven't had a nice roast in quite awhile. And the crock-pot makes such an easy one.

With the cooler weather the last few days, that sounds good. I'll make cornbread when I get home. Yep that should do the trick. I'm getting hungry just thinking about it. Better plan on a light lunch."

Chapter 23

Wednesday
31 Oct '07

"Surprise Mommy!" The twins laughed as they climbed on the big four-poster bed, "We got you presents and daddy is having Cook make a fancy breakfast even though it isn't Sunday, all because it's your birthday." Their voices were so jumbled together it was hard to tell who was saying what.

"All right, calm yourselves please." She said while trying to gather them up in a big hug. Looking towards the doorway she saw Jackson standing there laughing.

"Well, you could help you know?" She laughed.

"And spoil all their fun? Would I do that Jeanette?" was his reply. He came into the room scooping up James, as Jeanette managed to grab onto Jasmine.

"You two need to let your mother finish waking up and get dressed if you want to have that fancy breakfast." Jack said to the children, in a fake stern voice.

"Yes, Sir!" they both replied together, trying not to laugh.

"Mummy when were you born?" asked Jasmine.
"You already know the answer to that," said James.

"But I like to hear Her say it! With all the numbers."

"OK, I'll say it," chuckled Jeanette, "With ALL the numbers: 11-11-77 at 11:11 am. Now the two of you go get dressed, and we'll meet you down stairs for breakfast."

Jack set down James as Jeanette let go of Jasmine and the kids ran from the room. With a wink and a smile, Jack closed the door after them and returned to the bed.

"May I help you with your nightclothes?" He asked, untying her gown as he kissed her.

Kissing, they fell back together. Slowly Jackson unbuttoned the gown that Jeanette wore, one button at a time, kissing the bared skin as he went. He usually hated these high-necked styles, but this was fun. Under the chin...on the throat...that cute little cleft where the collarbones meet...where her locket hangs...at the top of her cleavage...deep in the middle...at the bottom. This could take hours, as he leisurely drew circles along the edges of her breasts.

Jeanette let out a low moan. She had been trying to pretend indifference, being still, with a haughty look on her face. But a woman could only resist so much. Every nerve she had was tingling. She knew it wasn't "Lady" like, but she finally took his head, and moved it to one exposed breast and said softly "Please!"

That's all he'd been waiting for; he lifted Jeanette up enough to remove her gown the rest of the way. "I want to see all of you," he murmured, caressing her body. "You keep getting more beautiful. More beautiful that when we first met. More beautiful than you were last year." He started kissing all those places he had been caressing, starting back at her breasts, and slowly circling to her navel, and then softly moving lower.

Walking down the stairs, Jeanette turned to Jackson and said, "I had the strangest dream last night. It was about one of those Colonial Natives. It was as if I were her, or something. I was seeing out of her eyes as her birthday celebration took place. It was very creepy. Then she died; she was run over by another savage on his horse. She said the oddest thing: "Beware 30...must warn the next."

156

"How very strange" replied Jack, "must have been all of Christopher's talking about his exploits during his visit."

"I would think so; it was certainly unsettling. I won't let it ruin the hunt, I did manage to block it out for a while there," she smiled as him, "yet it lingers."

The breakfast room was done up in creams and yellows to accent the east facing windows. Jeanette and Jackson were in full Hunting regalia, carrying their hats.

Conversation during the meal centered on the Birthday hunt. Who would be here, who couldn't make it and why. Which children were likely to attend, and how far they would be allowed to ride with the Hunt. Who would be Nanny this year? If Uncle Milton would get thrown by his horse this year? Always a great topic for debate.

After the dishes had been cleared and the tea had been refreshed, the children each picked up their presents and stood in front of their mother.

"Oh my, well who should go first?" Jeanette asked.

"I should, me! Me!" said James, jumping up and down. "I'm oldest!"

"BY only 5 minutes," replied Jasmine. "And you went first last year."

"Did Not!" whined James

"Yes you did, with that blue scarf you gave her. I remember!" Jasmine's answered.

"Oh, yeah...then I guess it's your turn. Well hurry up. You're taking too long."

"Here mum, I made this all by my self. It's why I've been in my room reading so much lately."

"Why thank you Jasmine. What pretty paper, where did you find it?" Jeanette asked.

"Pappa took us into town with him last week when you went to see Aunt Susan. It was all a big surprise." Jasmine giggled. *"Open it!"*

Carefully, Jeanette opened the package and found a knitted bed jacket all done in light blues and greens, with a purple ribbon tie. *"My! This is beautiful. Where did you learn to knit something this light and dainty? Not from me, that's for sure."*

"It's actually crochet, and Sally taught me. It's really quite simple, once you have the right needle and the right thin yarns. That was the hard part. Trying to explain to Pappa what I needed when he went to town last month. But he did quite well," she said in a very grown up tone.

"Yes I can see that, so did you! I'm very proud of you. This is so very soft. I can't wait to wear it tomorrow morning. Come here so I can give you a big hug." *And so saying, Jeanette moved her chair away from the table so she could embrace her daughter.*

"My turn now!" James said as he pushed his present between his mother and sister. *I made you something you really need. Not some silly old bed jacket. It's only a cape anyway."*

"It's not silly; I worked very hard on that. And mum needs it to keep her shoulders warm in the mornings when she has her tea up stairs. Mum, tell him it's not silly!" whined Jasmine.

"James it's a very lovely bed jacket. The cape style lets me wear it over any of my gowns. Don't be bratty, or you shall spend the day in your room, and not with the others on the Hunt."

"I'm sorry, and I'm sorry to you too Jasmine…Will you open mine now Mummy?"

"Of course, let me put this down first." Jeanette placed the bed jacket on the table, and looked at the presents in her lap.
"The big one first, then the other one, they go together."

"That's fine, let's see what we have here…" Jasmine said as she opened the larger package. *"…It's a? A? Let me take it out and get a good look at it."*

"It a Jewelry holder. See, it's a hand, and you put it on its base like this." James took the smooth hand shaped piece of wood from his mother, and twisted it into the flat piece he removed from the wrappings. The hand stood up on the table.

"The fingers are curved so you can put your necklaces on them, and the thumb has wholes for your earrings. And this shallow place in the base is for your hair combs. It's walnut, from that branch that fell behind the stables. And I made it all myself."

"Well, isn't that inventive, who showed you how to do all that?" An amazed Jeanette inquired. She ran her hand over the wood, feeling how wonderfully smooth it was.

"Mickey, in the stables. He does a lot of wood stuff. He let me use his knives and files and everything. He showed me how to find the right piece of wood for what we was, I mean were making. And how to make the base and the stand fit together, but still be able to come apart. This is for when you travel too. So you don't have to worry where everything gets to, it's all in one place. Isn't it super? Oh! Open the other one now!"

"All right James, calm yourself a bit, I'll open it now." Jeanette carefully opened the smaller package that was wrapped in tissue paper. *"Why, what a pretty Comb. Thank you James!"* she exclaimed as she pulled him into a hug. *"This will match the dress I'm wearing to the dance tonight. However did you know?"*

"Jasmine helped me on that one. She saw it when we all went to town. She knew I was looking for something to put on the tray. I thought this was pretty, and I had some money, 'cause my gift didn't really cost anything. I'm glad you like it."

"I really do. It's wonderful, as is the jewelry stand. I still can't believe the two of you are so grown up and so talented. Come here for another hug, both of you!"

"The guests are starting to arrive," Nancy announced, as she came in to finish tidying up the room, *"Mr. Groves has them by the gazebo as you requested. Your mounts are ready for you there as well."*

"Thank you Nancy," said Jeanette, "The children's presents took a while longer than we'd planned this morning. Could you please see that these other lovely gifts are taken to my room? I'll have to open them later."

Jeanette gave Nancy a smile over the twins' heads, so she'd let the other staff members know why their gifts hadn't been opened or acknowledged. It wouldn't do to slight anyone. They were the best help anywhere in the county, and she wouldn't want to lose them.

Over at the gazebo there were five riders with their horses so far, with others coming up the drive. They were expecting eight to ten families, with a few single friends and older relatives. A nice sized hunt, neither too big nor too small.

Peter, the groom, had Gentry and Queenie waiting, as well as, the two ponies. It was a lovely day for a hunt. The sun was shining, the birds were singing, there was a crisp feel to the air and the leaves crackled under the horse hooves. This was exactly what Jeanette had wished for in asking for good weather. She loved the feel of Queenie, her horse, as she cantered across the fields. The strength of her, the feeling of freedom, like she could go anywhere, be anyone. Ahhh...if only that was possible, well for a few short minutes, it was, and she enjoyed it immensely.

The fox made a dash out of the trees and across a corner of the Peterson's cornfield with the hounds right behind, baying out their song. The hunters moved to canter as they came to open ground, enjoying the faster pace after all the time walking through the trees. It wasn't a large field, so they didn't get up much speed as they came to a large tree over a brook on the edge of an apple orchard. The fox was giving them quite a merry chase. Half of the hunters swerved off to the right, to go the long way around the orchard. The other half jumped the log and continued up the path through up middle after the dogs.

She was in the second group, the last to make the jump. Queenie was halfway over the log when the horse shied throwing Jeanette off her back. Jeanette felt her leg snap when she hit the ground. She barely got a scream out, when Queenie fell back on her, crushing both legs and most of her lower half. She fainted. Queenie squirmed on the ground, then managed to stand.

160

Jackson heard Jeanette scream, whipped Gentry around, and was beside her in moments. He called to the others, who would come back as fast as they could, but just looking at her, he knew there was nothing anyone could do. Jeanette opened her eyes, smiled at Jack and whispered, "Beware 30...must warn the next!" She closed her eyes again and faded away.

Once again, Jade wakes up feeling that Jeanette is speaking directly to her. The warning is for her, and she better get the hint. She isn't as scared or worried as the day before, more resigned that these dreams aren't going to end until her birthday is over. Less than two weeks to go, she can survive this without going insane. She has to.

Jake was still home this morning, and still showering too. Well that'll help get any residual cobwebs out of her head, she thinks, and start her day off on a high note. She is halfway to the bathroom when there is a knock on her bedroom door.

"Mom, can I come in?" asks Jeremy in a very congested voice. "I don't feel so good."

"What's wrong sweetie?" she replies as she opens the door to a very sick looking child, "what hurts?"

"My throat hurts, my head hurts, I can't breathe, and it really hurts to swallow." Was the weak reply.

Putting the back of her hand on Jeremy's forehead, Jade immediately knows he is running a high fever. 101.5 or 102, she thinks as she herds him into the kids bathroom to get the thermometer. Sitting Jer on the closed toilet, she puts the gauge in his ear and presses the button for a reading. One hundred and one point nine, damn she's good.

Unfortunately, she's learned that little skill in temperature reading because of Jeremy's tendency to get strep throat. Feeling his neck, then looking down his throat with the little flashlight kept in the medicine cabinet for that reason, she knows he also has tonsillitis. Poor kid, he gets it quarterly, at least it seems that way. Military medicine doesn't consider a chronic history of strep throat and tonsillitis to be enough reason to remove those tonsils.

The fact that his tonsils are golf ball size when they are healthy, and that he snores like a freight train, doesn't interest them. They insist that a child has to have six cases of tonsillitis before they will remove the tonsils. The fact that he has 4, and another 3 or 4 cases of strep, where we catch it early enough to keep it from going into the tonsils are of no interest to the Navy Docs. "I love the military red tape," she thinks.

With the twins home sick for the day, so is Jade. She'll be spending the day getting caught up on a lot of odds and ends. Tonight being Halloween really makes Jeremy miserable. Jenifer promises to share her candy with her brother, as soon as he's healthy enough for it. "They could be so sweet some times, yeah usually when they were asleep," she laughs.

All right, off to the pediatric clinic for the latest round of antibiotics. But first, the phone calls. One to Alice, explaining that she will be home for the rest of the week. Jade should get a chance to do some work from the house this afternoon if the Sisters need her too. Jake'll stop by on his way home to pick up her working files so she doesn't get behind.

Then a call into the clinic to get an appointment time for both children. What one has today, the other will have tomorrow. Finally a call to the school, explaining why the kids are going to be out for a few days. As she expected, they aren't surprised, it's been making the rounds rather quickly in the last few days.

With a 10:00 AM appointment, she has enough time to get her shower, grab some coffee and an English muffin, and read the front page of the paper, which usually waits till she gets home in the evenings. Without too much fuss she manages to bundle both kids into the car and off they drive to see the Doc.

Having twins gives you twice the chance to visit the pediatric clinic, and they are well known. The front office staff are all civilians, and have worked in the clinic for quite some time. The nurses and doctors are Navy Officers and rotate through every 2-3 years. You

162

never are sure which doctor will be on duty, or even still on station if the kids have been healthy for a while.

Jade is glad to see Doctor Sheridan is still here; she's the twins favorite Doc so far. Dr. Kim, as she prefers everyone to call her, talks to the kids like they are real people, not some deaf mutes that aren't even there. The respect she gives the children is returned double by their parents.

When she comes into the exam room after the nurse has taken both Jeremy and Jenyfer's vitals, she asks the kids what is wrong.

"Jer has Strep." Jeny states.

"I can talk for myself," snaps Jer wincing a little as he does so. "My throat hurts a lot, especially when I talk. I have a fever. And I can't swallow more than water. So yep it's strep, again! Are they ever going to take my tonsils out?"

"I'm sorry Jeremy, but that isn't my choice. I did put in the request again, and it was rejected. But I have lined up an allergist that is interested in seeing you. She might be able to make a case for the constant illnesses being a form of autoimmune illness. You might be allergic to your tonsils. Then they could be taken out. What do you think of that?" Dr. Kim asked.

"Great, when can I see him? Or her?"

"Not until you're healthy. Let me have a look, but if your mom says she saw the puss, then I believe her. We'll do the throat cultures, put you both on the antibiotics for ten days. And then see you back in two weeks to make sure you're really over this. If you are all clear, I can set up your appointment with Dr. Shirley. I think you'll really like her."

"Okay," says Jer. Jeny just nods, as does Jade. They both know this drill way too well.

Chapter 24

Thursday
1 Nov '07

"Liebhabering? Are you awake? Johanna?" Her husband whispered in her ear as she was slowly becoming conscious. "I'd like to give you your first birthday gift," he said with a twinkle in his voice.

"Not that again…Jarvis, you give me the same thing every year." She replied in mock annoyance, but couldn't stifle her laughter as he started to tickle her. Turning her gently, they'd just started to kiss when the door burst open, and 2 kids jumped on the bed.

"I told you she was awake." The little girl said, half-playful, half-bratty.

"But Vater said to wait until HE opened the door," replied her brother, not really whining.

"Well I guess it's too late for that now. Come on kids, lets all kiss Mutter 30 times for her 30th Geburtstag!" So saying, they all ganged up on Johanna and kissed her everywhere they could manage. On her face, her neck, her arms, her hands; it became a wrestling match.

"Enough! Peace! I surrender! Let me up and I'll make you all some breakfast. You two go and get dressed, and we'll be down in a bit. Jan, be my big boy and put some more coals on the fires, but don't smother them. Joselyn, please get the table ready for breakfast. Ich Liber Dich Alles!"

*The twins, scampered out of the room, closing the door as they went .
Johanna turned back to her Jarvis. "Now about that present? I think
you were about to unwrap it?"*

Jarvis came back to the bed and climbed back under the covers.

*"I think I can manage to find something to amuse you Schatzi, I know
you like kisses here..." He said, trailing kisses up her arm towards her
throat. "And here..." now kissing behind her ears, and nibbling on her
ear lobes, "and here..." covering her mouth in a passionate kiss.*

*Jarvis was quite a kisser, each one even deeper than the last; it was as if
he was trying to climb inside her heart, as it was melting into his. Both
sets of hands were removing clothes, and caressing warm skin. Petting
and playing, while the kisses continued to evolve into a total union of
breaths and souls. Eventually the kisses started traveling to other body
parts, after all everything tasted so good. And taste they did, from their
nose to their toes, and various favorite spots in between.*

*Johanna cooked up wursts, and potato cakes. There was kaffe and
milch for das kinder. Dark brot, and butter, fresh melone, and
erdbeeres, in September! "Melons and strawberries, speak English!
Johanna, coffee and milk, English!" she said aloud. "The children
need the English!"*

*"And so do I, living in the big city of New York," she thought. "I need
to speak better to do my shopping." The endless supply of foods
delighted her in New York. She could find almost anything, all year
round. "What a great city. To be sure, it had its problems, yet it was so
good to us. Jarvis has a good job. The children go to a good school,
right down the block. And the ease with which I can get all the
shopping done, just great."*

"Fruhstuck is ready!" She called. "I mean breakfast!"

*As she walked into the dining room, Jarvis and the children shouted
"Alles Gute Zum Geburtstag! Happy Birthday Muter!"*

*Right where she had planned to place the platter of food were gaily-
wrapped packages. Jarvis took the platter, "Here let me take that. You*

166

sit, and we'll serve you today." He said smiling, and placed the platter on the sideboard.

Jan pulled out her chair and Joselyn placed a ring of flowers in her hair as Johanna sat. "This is all lovely!" She said. "I wasn't expecting you to go to this much trouble."

"YOU only turn 30 once." Jarvis grinned. "You're old as me now."

"Only for 2 weeks Vater." Joselyn laughed, as Jan poured the Kaffe. "You'll be OLD again in 2 weeks"

"Thank you for that reminder kleiner madchen, I appreciate it." Jarvis picked up Joselyn and swung her around once, putting her right back in place.

"My turn," piped up Jan.

"I wouldn't forget you kleiner hosenmatz." Jarvis grabbed Jan and swung him harder, and plopped him down in his seat. "Time to eat before everything gets cold."

As they enjoyed the breakfast, Johanna said to Jarvis, "the dream I had night before...the Indian frau? This night I have a new one. The woman was in England. Was riche frau, a rich woman. Her 30 birthday also, she dies when they go on big Fuchsjagd. The foxhunting, for the rotfuchs. The pferd, the horse, she rides misses the big tree, and vom pferd fallen, she falls from the horse. The back, I think, it breaks, and more things. But she says the Beware 30...must warn the next! And she has by birth date. What does it mean Jarvis?"

"I have no knowing, it is very strange. We should talk more when the kinder are not here. They listen too well."

"This is true," replied Johanna, "Help me with the plates; I made applekuchen for a treat."

After the meal was cleaned up, Johanna asked to move the presents to the front room. She enjoyed sitting on the large sofa that backed to the big picture window overlooking the street.

How pretty the paper she had pasted on the walls was in the morning light. The two large chairs by the fireplace were her mother's, the lace curtains his. A nice blend of the old world and this new one.

Sitting in the middle of the sofa, with one child on either side, Johanna said, "Now we are ready for the gifts!" and she started laughing.

"What is so funny muter?" asked Jan, "Why do you laugh?"

"The English, the word gift in English is to mean present. But in German, the word pronounced like gift means poison. So I said it was time for poison. There are a few of the words like that; I cannot help but to laugh."

"I think I understand. Will you open whatever they are now?"

"Yes, I am ready now; let's see what surprises my lovely family has for me."

"Jan may be first," said Joselyn.. "I went first last year."

"How do you remember?" asked Jan as he handed his mother a prettily wrapped box.

"I just do, I think it comes from being older," she laughed, "mostly from being a girl."

Johanna opened her gift to find a nice rectangular box with a carved lid. "My, how pretty, where did you get this?" She asked.

"I made it for you," answered Jan with pride. " Vater has been showing me how to carve the top. In school I took the class. I made the box. I hope you use it for your jewelry. I know you have some cloth to line it with. I just didn't know how to do it."

"I will do that. It is very lovely Jan, thank you so much. Come give me a kiss." Johanna hugged and kissed her son with much pride showing on her face.

"My turn!" smiled Joselyn, "I made my present also." She handed her mother a soft package, wrapped in paper, with many bows.

"Look at the pretty bows, Why so many of them?" asked Johanna laughing.

"There are five bows," answered Joselyn. "2 kinder times 5 bows times the 10 years we are alive equals 30 years for you! I didn't have the ribbon for 30 bows, and the package is not that big. So I made a way to have a number that had a meaning."

Jan just looked at her, "I would never have thought this. How do you do so well with the numbers? I think you will be in a bank when you grow up. You are just to fast with all the numbers."

"Numbers are just easy for me, you are the one who remembers all the dates and who did what in the history. I can never get them all straight. I think when we were made twins we each got half the brain." She laughed and the others joined in. "Now you can open the package Muter."

Johanna ripped the paper to find a lovely scarf and mittens. They were blue and green in a very pretty design. "Joselyn, did you crochet these by yourself? They are beautiful, and so warm."

"I do not have the hat finished. It is harder, because I wanted to make one that is fancy. I'm not so sure I will be able; I hope you will help me. I'm sorry I know you should not have to work on your own present. But it is very hard." Joselyn was almost in tears as she admitted this to her mother.

"Come her little one," cooed Johanna, "These are wonderful, I know the hats can be very hard. I would be very happy to help you. It is good for me to take the time to crochet as well. My fingers need the exercise." With hugs and kisses, she had Joselyn smiling in moments.

"And now for my present," said Jarvis. We must go to the store to see it. It could not be ready until this morning."

"What is it Vater?" asked Jan. "Will you tell us, and only make Muter wait?"

"No!" Jarvis said. "It will be a surprise for everyone. Let's get the coats, Johanna you can use your new scarf and mittens. It is very cold today, and the snow is to fall. But we only walk a few streets."

Everyone bundled up and set off to the mystery store for Johanna's present. It turned out to be to a jewelry store that Jarvis led them. "What is this?" asked Johanna, "I don't need any jewelry."

"Come," he said, leading the way into the store. "I'm here to pick up my purchase." Jarvis told the clerk behind the counter, handing him a slip of paper.

Reading it the clerk replied, "I have it right here Mr. Waggoner, did you want it gift wrapped?"

"No, I would like her to wear it home please," he answered. The clerk brought over a small box and handed it to Jarvis. Opening it towards Johanna, he got down on one knee and said, "I could not offer you the engagement ring when we wed. And for these 13 years, all you have is your wedding band. Now I am giving you the engagement ring, so I ask again 'Will you marry me?'"

Johanna was overwhelmed with emotions. The simple gold band with 1/3-carat solitaire diamond was beautiful, more beautiful than anything she had ever seen. But her big strong husband, on his knee, in the store was just too much. She began to cry as she said, "Ja, I will marry you, again and again and again! I love you, you wonderful man; now get up before you hurt your self. You are embarrassing me."
Jarvis stood and put the ring on Johanna's finger then gave her the biggest hug in the world. The grin on his face went from ear to ear, and threatened to split it in two. How he could be so happy he'll never understand, he just knew it all came from his Johanna.

The kinder were clamoring around to see the ring, as they were getting a bit rowdy, the family moved out to the street. Enjoying the way the ring shone in the sunlight, Johanna smiled even brighter. "We should be getting home," she said. "The kinder still have to go to the school after the lunch. And even if it is my birthday, the cleaning must be done." The happy family started their three-block walk home.

When they were crossing the first intersection, a carriage came racing around the corner. The horse looked frightened, its eyes wide and not seeing anything. The driver of the carriage was calling for the horse to stop, and yelling for people to move out of the way. Jarvis and Jan were most of the way across and out of danger, but Joselyn and Johanna were in the middle of the street.

As Johanna yelled to run, Joselyn froze in terror, staring at the horse running right at her. Johanna moved to her daughter and shoved her aside, just as the horse came upon her, there was no chance for Johanna to save herself. The horse knocked her down and continued right over her. Only two of the carriage wheels hit her, but it was enough. As Jarvis and the children ran back to her, she looked up at them and said, 'Beware 30...must warn the next!" She died in their arms.

Jade isn't sure what the purpose of these repeating dreams are. Nothing has changed, and always the deaths, always the warning. As if, she'll ever forget that by now. It is permanently etched in her brain. Only ten more days to go, she can last that long she is sure, she hopes so anyway.

Johanna has definitely been looking directly at her. No doubt about it, directly at her. What is she supposed to do? It's not like Jade can stop the horse. A little late to stop her death, what else can she do? She isn't about to have a séance and try to evoke the women's spirits. So what else is left? Damn I wish I knew, she thinks in frustration.

Work is busy for a Thursday; she doesn't even get a break this afternoon. Her next-door neighbor Debbie, the mother of the kids' best friends is babysitting. Her two kids also have strep, and are on antibiotics, so they figure only one mother should have to stay home. Debbie has a big presentation Friday, and asked if Jade could watch her two then, so Jade went in today. Now she's regretting that decision. She knows that Alice and Alicia would have been totally swamped without her. So she does feel a bit better at having saved them from a total day of hell.

She gets home and finds that she's forgotten to defrost the chicken she is planning on cooking for dinner. She hates the way the microwave defrosts it. Time to rethink, not something she's good at when she's this mentally exhausted. Just as she is about to open a package of macaroni and cheese for the kids, Jake comes home.

"What are you making?" he asks innocently.

"Why do you want to know?" she snaps at him. "You'll eat whatever you're given."

"Ouch, I guess you had one of those days, want to go out for pizza?" he asks gently, giving her a hug.

"That sounds heavenly; it's been a bitch and a half today. I'd love to do pizza, and you know the kid's will be thrilled. Thanks for the save. I just couldn't think. I love you, you know." Jade smiles a bit sheepishly.

"It's my job to be here to save you, remember. I wouldn't mind a pizza myself you know," he admits. They gather up the kids and drive to their favorite pizza parlor. It's amazing how quickly the new generation antibiotics act on Jeremy's strep throat. In just over 36 hours you can barely tell he was sick, until he actually got around to eating.

Once they order, and give the kids quarters to play the video games, Jade takes a good look at Jake and can see he's upset. "What's up Hun, you look like you've lost your best friend? She asks.

"I'm afraid I might," is his reply. "Lewis got a call today; Commander Johnson's wife in Germany is in end stage breast cancer. They are shipping home immediately, this weekend. The other officer up for the slot just found out his wife's pregnant; she's had some medical problems in the past, miscarried twice at the end of the second trimester and can't go overseas, that leaves us. I can't believe in a few weeks we've gone from 25% to 100%. Please don't just sit there, say something."

Jade is just staring at him, her mouth hanging slightly open. "We're moving to England, by New Years. This can't be happening," she thinks.

"What else is going to happen? Yikes!!!!"

Taking a deep breath, she smiles at Jake and says, "England will be nice in the spring, and I understand they don't get snow in London, it's too warm. Now's a good time for the kids to go too, they're old enough to enjoy it, and still remember it when they get older. The change in school systems won't be a problem, as it can in high school. I think timing for the family is going to work out just fine.

"You're not mad?" asks a surprised Jake.

"Why would I be mad? I knew this might happen I've had a few weeks to give it some thought, and I really like the idea of a few years in England. I think four is a bit too many, but I'll probably be the one who wants you to extend when the time comes to move back. I think this is going to be fun."

Jade feels she should be getting an Oscar for this performance, but supporting her husband is her first priority. And she will get used to the idea, will probably really enjoy herself once she gets over there. It's just all this dream stuff that has her so on edge. Yeah, England will be an adventure. Jade never bypasses an adventure.

Chapter 25

Thursday
2 Nov '07

Lilac Wolf is walking along the river talking to Jade, "From this side of the Great River I see the wishes of 'He Who Never Dies'. He tells me that my daughter's daughter of many times will save me from walking this life and send me to the great beyond. I look in your eyes and I see my little Turquoise chick. She saw a Wolf, like me, upon her womanhood. Very strong totem, very strong name. She mated with a great warrior, had many kits, and became the great Wise Woman.

I watched her grow as the flower grows, but always with the thorn piercing her heart. I was that thorn. She lived her days missing what she could no longer have. When she went to her final rest, I was not there, for I am still here. I need my tribe, I miss my days, help me to return to my youth, to my happy days.

I warn the ones, born the day of my birth. They did not know me. There must be blood. It must be you. Help me. Beware 30...must warn next"

Jade wakes shaking, this was so very different, Lilac Wolf had been speaking directly to her. "She said I'm her granddaughter. I don't know her. We don't have any Indians in our family tree, do we?"
"Are you speaking to me sweetie?" asks Jake from the bathroom.

"No, just to myself," Jade answers as she walks towards him to explain this latest twist. "Today, or rather last night, Lilac Wolf spoke directly to me. She said that she was my grandmother; many times removed, from Turquoise chick, or rather Turquoise Wolf as she becomes. That she'd tried to warn the others, Jeanette and Johanna, but they hadn't understood. Only blood could lift whatever curse she was under, and that I was that blood."

"Very odd, I don't remember any Native American blood in your family. Sounds like it would have to be on your mother's side right?"

"That's how I took her meaning. Mom's mom was from Kentucky, Great Grandma from Virginia, as was her family for generations. The known tree only goes back to the Civil War. Before that, the knowledge of the distaff side is long gone. I guess with the tribes moving back and forth from Virginia thru North Carolina to South Carolina, one of the early Gents could have taken a native wife, or adopted a child. I'll never know."

"Do you realize I could be related to all three women? Mom was English/Irish. The English being from the early settlers, Lilac Wolf lived during the French and Indian wars. The English were fighting on the Indian's side, so they could oust the French. Easy enough to end up with a squaw wife. They were a light-skinned tribe so no one would know.

I'm not sure where Jeanette comes from, either Mom's Irish or Dad's Scot. Grandma Neison's family was landed-gentry in Scotland at one point, until the wars with England over independence. I can see the too families meeting and a marriage happening between a daughter and a son. We don't know what happened to Jasmine, or her children.

Dad was half German too. That would explain Johanna, and I seem to recall Great-Grandma Hartsig saying that her mother died when she was a little girl. I don't know what her first name is; all anybody called her was grandma. I think I was eight or nine when she died, so my memory is fuzzy. I'll ask dad when I talk to him. However, we both know how he is on names, and remembering that type of thing." Jade laughs softly at the thought of her dad.

176

That's a problem for a different day, she thinks. Time to get started with today.

Chapter 26

Friday
9 Nov '07

Jeanette sat at her breakfast table, drinking tea, as she talked to Jade. "You remind me of my Jasmine. Her smile, her grace, her talent with others. I wish I could have been there to help her become a woman. I simply watched. She became quite a beauty, married well, and had a wonderful life. It was her second daughter, Jean, that moved to Scotland. They named her after me. She is your ancestor, and is the one who is the blood tie for us."

Jean was very smart. Her husband died young, leaving her with a large estate and three children. Instead of re-marrying, as most women of the time would have, Jean ran the estate by herself. She did such a good job that when each child got married, she gave them an estate the size of the one she started out with.

You are my hope. I am tired of watching my family live and die over and over with no rest for me. Please understand what we do. Hear us. We need you. I need you. I want to go to my rest. To be with my family again. Please help us, remember…Beware 30…must warn the next."

"So now I'm the great white hope," mutters Jade waking from yet another, dissimilar dream. She realizes she had some comfort in knowing the stories behind the dreams. Jade had gotten used to the pattern of the three dreams every week. Yet this week there was no Monday or Tuesday night dream. She was confused by the lack of them, and even more so by these new one-on-one encounters. What is she to do to break this curse? So far, nobody has mentioned that.

"It would be nice to have some DETAILS!" she says aloud. "I'd like to know what I seem to have been born to do. At least pass down a decoder ring or something. Align the stars with the answer, just give me a clue will you guys? Okay? Well I'm going out to enjoy my day.

Jade has today off; actually, she has the whole four-day weekend off. Saturday is the Marine Corps Birthday Ball. Always "THE" premier event on her social calendar. She is taking today to pamper herself, part of Jake's birthday present to her. A wonderful day at Henri's Day Spa. "Le Stone Massage" her favorite, a facial, a manicure and a pedicure. With a luncheon, and time in the sauna, steam room and the soothing relaxation room between procedures. It is a whole day experience, and the perfect present.

The hot stone massage is the greatest experience since chocolate in Jade's opinion, maybe even better than sex. Okay, not sex, and chocolate might be pushing it. However, the way she's been feeling lately, it's damn close. Over ninety minutes of a soothing massage done by using polished lava rocks that have been heated in a scented water bath.

First, oil is applied in a penetrating massage, to get the skin softened and the muscles loosened. Then the stones are used one or two at a time, to apply a deep, warming massage over every part of your body, except the genitals and breasts of course. The stones hold the heat a very long time, and the relaxation achieved in one of these sessions is unbelievable. You just want to melt off the table.

Jake is such a love. He's even let her sleep in, gotten the kids up and out, and reset the alarm to give her plenty of time to eat a light breakfast, and get to the Spa. With that thought in mind, she gives a long slow stretch, and lazily climbs out of bed.

Maybe I should live like this more often, Miss pampered princess. She'll hold off on the shower, she needs to take one at the spa anyway. Both the Hot Stone and the Facial will make an oily mess of her hair, so she'll end up showering again before bed.

Jade grabs her navy and white jogging suit out of her dresser, along with a tank and sports bra. She knows it's best to wear loose, baggy clothes. She tosses a pair of sandals into her tote bag, so the polish on her toes will dry without being ruined, checks that her swim suit is still there for the sauna and steam rooms, and makes sure she has her gift certificate, and membership card. She gets the monthly newsletter, and discounts on any products and services she purchases while there.

When Jade enters Henri's Day Spa it's like old home week, greetings fly from every corner as various technicians welcome her back or wish her a happy birthday. You'd think she'd worked there for years and has just come back from vacation, the way they were treating her. Sure, she is a good tipper, but that's just the way the clients are treated at Henri's, like family.

Jade isn't normally the full package girl. She will save up for her quarterly "Le Stone," or if a formal dining event occurs, she gets her nails done. This is her first VIP all day package. She is so excited she feels like a kid.

Chapter 27

Saturday
10 Nov '07

Johanna was in her living room, sitting on the sofa she loved. She offered Jade a cup of Kaffe as she said, "You remind me of my Joselyn, very smart, very organized, very proud. Your hair is the same auburn color and you stand like her. I know you don't remember her, you were too young, yet you are the child of my child's, child's, child. You are my blood."

I remember the small girl who would read to her. Tell my Joselyn her dreams of traveling the world, seeing all the places in her books. Now I need her help for me to travel to the heavens to be with my family. I wish to rest. This is just too hard. Please, you are our only hope.

Those before me could not help, it was to be this way, we know not why. Yet, it is for you to break the curse. It is a great burden, but we are here to help. Just trust in the love of the family. Beware 30...must warn the next."

Could Joselyn really be her great, grand mother? Jade wondered. She did remember reading to the little old lady, when the family went to visit.

These were usually big family deals, with all the aunts and uncles and cousins. Lots of people in Granny's little house, everybody talking at once, and nobody really listening.

Great-grandma would sit with the adults for about an hour, and then she'd go to her sewing room and sit in her gigantic rocker. It was easily big enough for two, probably two daddies. So it held Granny and her just right. There were big green cushions on it, to match the curtains in the room, and a large afghan that Granny said she had crocheted when she was a teenager.

They would snuggle up all cozy and Jade would read to her from whatever book she was currently reading. It never occurred to the child that a 90-something woman wasn't really interested in the adventures of Nancy Drew and the Black Stallion. Or that hearing the middle chapters of a book were a very hard way to understand one. Jade always did her best to read very clearly and precisely, and to explain the plot so far, so Granny wouldn't get too lost.

They would discuss all the different places in the books, about Granny's parents coming over from Germany, and about her childhood in New York. How could she have forgotten?

It sure looked like this was all real. That the women were her ancestors and that she had to figure out how to save them. If she only had a clue.

The Marine Corps Birthday Ball is one of the most formal dining events thrown in this country, and around the world. It is held on the anniversary of the inception of the U. S. Marine Corps, November 10th, every year. It starts approximately one week before the date when a Marine in formal dress and white gloves shows up at your door with your invitation. That usually gets the neighbors talking. When was the last time anyone hand delivered an invitation to you?

At the Ball, all the Marine Officers and Enlisted men are dressed in their formal Dress Blue Uniforms. They wear their swords and gloves. There is a precise order and agenda for the first half of the evening. From the presentation of the colors, to the honoring of the oldest and the youngest marine in the room. Like any Military Dining-out, there are toasts to the President, to the first Lady, to the Major General of the Marine Corps, to the Flag, to any visiting dignitaries, and the list goes on and on.

They have a formal presentation of the beef, to be sure it is acceptable to eat, and fines for a variety of real and imagined infractions. They cut the birthday cake with a saber, then present the first two pieces to the aforementioned eldest and youngest Marines. The retiring of the colors, signals the end of the formal portion of the evening.

As scripted and formal as the first half of the evening is, the second is nothing short of a riot, well almost. Fill a banquet hall with a few hundred Marine officers and a handful of Navy and Army Officers, supply them with free liquor, add music, and before you know it people are dancing on the tables, and lying on the floor. The Marines are some of the hardest working people in the military, and they are some of the hardest partiers too.

Jade wears a jewel toned jade green dress, with spaghetti straps and 2-inch matching heels. Her auburn hair is swept up in a half french bun that falls out on one side looking accidentally sexy. She's the mother of two, but she doesn't have to advertise it tonight. She loves to dance, and never has to worry about a partner.

Jake's office mate is the Marine that invited them to the Ball, though they knew half a dozen others that would have extended the invitation. Tom is single and hasn't bothered with a date, so Jade dances with him quite often. Jake has a bad knee from college soccer and sits out every other dance, but this doesn't keep him from having a good time, and it doesn't slow Jade down much either.

There are always formal portraits taken. For some of these guys, this is the only time they will wear this uniform all year. With the new digital equipment, you get to proof your photos right away, and can decide if you want to order any additional ones for your Christmas cards. If you don't like your shots, then you can just start over and pose until there's a picture you like. The digital age is so wonderful.

This year seems especially sweet as the couple realizes they won't be anywhere close to a Marine base next year. There is no way of knowing how many are assigned to the Liaison office, and if they even manage to throw a small party or not. As the evening goes on it begins to take on a sad, nostalgic feel, so Jade suggests it's time to leave.

Walking from the Marriott Ballroom in downtown Annapolis, they stop and look around, taking in all the lights and sounds, knowing it's for the last time on this occasion.

Chapter 28

Sunday
11 Nov '07

She stands looking into an antique mirror standing in the corner of her bedroom. It is beautiful: three sided, floor length, carved oak, with an intricate oak leaf and acorn motif along the top edge. Jade knows it is the prettiest piece of furniture she's ever seen. Looking back at her are the three women: Lilac Wolf, Jeanette Wright and Johanna Waggoner. They can all see her. She is looking out with all four sets of eyes, and it's very disconcerting. She hasn't noticed before how similar their faces are. How much they look like her. Upon closer inspection, they look almost exactly like her. How very odd.

She isn't surprised to see them. It is strange that they are all together. She's surprised at the appearance of the mirror in the corner of her room. It feels right to have her family here. Maybe they will finally explain how to break this curse.

Smiling she looks at each woman in turn, and then addresses them as a whole. "Who's going to explain how I'm to 'Beware 30?' You've warned me, but what is next? What haven't you told me? I know there has to be more to it than this. So what's the catch? I know you are all my grandmothers, many times removed. Haven't a clue what that means. I know you aren't trying to hurt me, that I'm supposed to help you break some curse or something, but a hint would really help here.

You all may be able to get inside of my head, but I'm having no luck getting inside yours. Any chance of one of you filling me in on the big secret? Or giving me the key to unlock the code or whatever I need to free you all, and let me go on with my life in peace and quiet."

They just stood and stared out at her.

"Come on guys, I'm asking really nicely. Just a bit of a hint, maybe a word or two."

As one they said, "We are you. Beware 30, or YOU will be next!"

"**NO!!!**" Jade wakes screaming again. "You can't be me. I'm me!" She's shaking and starring wide-eyed into space. Hearing her yell, Jake comes running in from the dressing room and wraps his arms around her.

"What's wrong Jade? I'm right here. Calm down honey. Tell me what's wrong. Was it the dreams again? You're Ok, I've got you."

"They were here, in the room. They said they are me, and I am going to be next if I don't lift the curse. I'm so scared. I've never been so cold. It is as if ice is pouring over me. I don't think I'll ever be warm again," she whimpers.

Grabbing the spread and pulling it around her, Jake pulls Jade onto his lap and just holds her as she calms down. "It's OK now sweetie, I've got you. I won't let anyone hurt you. Just hold on to me, and I'll warm you up."

Slowly Jade returns to her senses. Her heart slows, her shivering stops, and she smiles weakly up at Jake. "You must think I'm an idiot, totally freaked by this dream, especially after all the others. All they did was say a few words. I'm sorry for making such a big thing out of this."

"Don't be silly, we both know you're supposed to break their curse, with no idea of how. Now to find out that if you don't you'll be condemned like they are. I'm damn freaked myself.

If you're feeling up to it, why don't you go take a hot shower? The kids are planning breakfast in bed for you, and I'm sure you want to look you're best."

"That sounds like a good idea. I think I can get up now...I love you so much! Thanks again for the rescue. I owe you one, Ok... many, but a Big One for this." Jade says as she rises from Jakes lap and unwinds herself from the covers.

"I'm sure I can think of a way to pay me back," he replies with a touch of a leer, as he watches her walk into the bathroom. She's still a bit unsteady, but at least she can move on her own, that's a good sign.

"I wish I knew what was going on," he thinks. "How can I help her? This has been so crazy, and I feel so useless. What more can I do? How can I make it stop? I don't want it to ruin her Birthday. Damn it!"

After hearing her get into the shower, he quietly leaves the room. As he walks down the hall, the phone rings. Grabbing the wireless quickly off the hall table, he answers it. It's Alice, asking if Jade can work. Alicia is extremely ill, and they really need Jade. It will only be for the four hours. Alice will open and close. Jade will get time and a half, she begs. And a second 1/2-day over the holidays when she needs it.

They must really be hurting for Alice to offer both Time and Pay, thinks Jake as he wanders back to the bedroom with the phone in his hand.

"Honey," he calls. "Alice is on the phone, she needs you to work today. Alicia is sick, sounds like she has that vertigo again." Jake hands Jade the phone, giving her a kiss on the forehead, and a big smile. "You can always say no," he suggests. Even though he knows that isn't really an option for her.

"Jade, thank you so much for coming in...I know it's your birthday and all. Alicia is just so sick she can't leave the bathroom. You know how Sundays are this time of year. You'd think everyone would be gone for the long weekend or something. But I'm just too afraid to be left all alone here today. I'll make it up to you," Alice rattles it all off in one long breath the minute Jade walks in the door.

It's five minutes until Noon, five minutes until opening the Agency for the day. Jade can already see three people waiting by the door. "It's a good thing I came," Jade thinks. "There is no way Alice can handle this, she's too distracted by Alicia being sick. Besides, it's only four hours and overtime at that. Happy Birthday to Me!"

Jade turns on her computer, puts away her purse, and walks over to flip the sign and open the door. Let the day begin. It is a busy one indeed, both Alice and Jade work non-stop for those four hours. They book two holiday cruises, three Disney spring break packages, and arrange the initial planning for a wedding / honeymoon package on St. Thomas. Not bad for half a days work.

Most of the bookings are clients that have been in before and are finalizing their plans and making deposits or payments. But there is one couple that walked-in out of the blue, and they need a lot of coaching to get them to narrow down what it is they are looking for.

The D'Angelo's start by telling Jade that they are planning a fifth anniversary trip in February. They actually got married the first week in May, but wanted to be out of the area, and somewhere warm in the middle of the winter.

Jade asks them what they like to do? Play golf? Scuba Dive? Water Ski? Lay about on the Beach? Shop? Gamble? After every one they say, "yeah, we like to do that." She tries not to get frustrated, but they aren't exactly helpful.

Giving up on that tact, she asks what area they want to visit, Mexico, the Caribbean, or Europe? "I don't know, they all sound like fun," is their answer.

Then she comes to the money question. Do you have a budget in mind? Any idea what price range you would like to look in? "No, we have plenty of money, that's not the problem. We only have 2-3 weeks though, so it can't be too far, cause Dedee here don't like to fly." Just great, now what is she going to do?

In a flash of brilliance, she gives them brochures on Florida, including the auto train. They can drive their cars to the station in Lorton, Virginia. Take the train ride over night, booking one of the cabins for two. They'll have their car when they get to Florida, and Dedee won't have to fly. Plus they will save on the cost of renting a car. Jade will book them into hotels wandering down the east coast of Florida, all the way to Key West. Then they will drive back up the west coast and visit the Tampa and Orlando areas for a few nights each. Before driving back to the train station for the return trip to Virginia.

They are thrilled, and booked on the spot. It takes a bit to confirm their berth on the train, Sunday is the Auto train's busiest day for phone calls, but once that was in place, everything else is easy. Jade really earns her commission on this one. She just knows that they are going to be very needy clients. Constantly calling her for every bit of information, she has already given them, or they can find out very easily on line.

The day is finally over. As Alice does the bookwork, Jade types a quick email to Dave to tell him that she is related to Lilac Wolf, and have him stop by for details. As she hits the send button Jade hears the sound of a loud car engine.

She looks up as a red Mustang convertible comes crashing through the glass door and lands on her desk, crushing her between the car, the desk and the wall. She manages to scream for Alice before she passes out.

Alice comes running into the room as she is calling 911, having heard the crash. Not that you can miss it in that small a space. She runs toward Jade, but can't reach her. She can't get to the car door without pulling on it. There looks to be a teenager in the car, and he doesn't look conscious either.

"What is the nature of your emergency?" asks the operator.

"I'm at 121 Main Street, downtown Annapolis. A car just crashed through the front door. Jade's trapped under it, I think she's dead, and there's a lot o' blood. And the driver's hurt too. Please hurry!"

"We already have the fire department and the emergency squad on their way. Someone already called it in. Just try to stay calm, and they will be there in a minute. You should be hearing the sirens by now."

"Yes I do. Thank you! I've got to go. I've got to call Jake. I've got to call Alicia." As Alice hangs up three men in uniforms come through the doorway.

"What do we got?" the lead one asks.

"Jade's pinned under the car, she looks dead. And the boy in the car hasn't moved since I came out of the back room. I was going to try the door, but I was afraid if I did anything it would hurt Jade." Alice explains.
"You did the right thing, Ma'am. We'll take it from here."

Stevens, you're on the boy, check those car doors. Davis you're on the gear. We'll need collars, and back boards, and get the Squad in here. We need to stabilize this thing before we can do anything. Get the LT moving now!"

"Right on it, Sarge," replies Davis, an EMT, as he hustles out the door.

Sarge walks around the far side of everything, and manages to slide between the sidewall and the edge of the car, just reaching Jade.

"She has a pulse, and she's breathing," He calls to Alice. "Looks like the desk took most of the weight, and managed to protect her some. Most of the blood seems to be cuts from the glass."

"Thank God!" She says as she falls into her chair in relief. "Oh No! I haven't called Jake." She opens her phone and places the call she was dreading a bit less, now that she knows Jade is alive.

192

"The passenger front door is unlocked and open," calls Stevens, "I can see that he's breathing. Seems pretty cut up, nose is bleeding, a lot of cuts, but no obvious breaks or major bleeds. Want me to go up or wait?"

Just then, the Rescue Squad rushes in. "Hey Sarge, you here? It's Lieutenant Brown, with Greene and White. That's your rig ain't it? Where are you?"

Sarge calls from his spot by Jade. "We've got one wedged over here, and a driver in the car. Get 'er stabilized as fast as you can, so we can get 'em moving, LT."

"I hear you Sarge, but where are you?" asked Lt. Brown, looking around, as Green and White went back out for equipment.

"Over here, in the corner, under the front of the car. Patient's hanging on, but just barely."

"Understood, we're moving."

Brown and Green come in carrying cribbing. The wood pieces that look a lot like 4x4s, they stack together to make a safe support for the car to rest on. A lot like the old Lincoln Logs toys. The men stack them on each side, in front of the rear tires. Once they have as much of the weight as possible on them, they deflate both rear tires. How they didn't blow is anyone's guess?

Now Stevens, the Jr. Paramedic, climbs into the car from the open door and moves over to his patient. Gently slipping the collar around the teen's neck, he does a quick evaluation. No obvious bones broken, nose was broken, and bleeding profusely. Reaching into the box he brought along, he opens gauze squares and tapes them in place. He cleans up the boy's face, and places steri-strips on a few of the deeper gashes to try to stem the bleeding.

As he is tending to the other cuts and gashes, Stevens notices the squad has the floor covered with all their extraction equipment. They are in a heated debate about the best way to cut the ragtop off the car.

193

"Hey guys," he calls, "how about if I do this?" He leans over and pushes the button that opens the top. He smiles at them as it recedes into its nest. The looks they give him are not polite.

"Hand me up a back board." He yells over to Davis. "I'm going to lay this seat down, and cut the seatbelt. We can pull him onto the board, as we move him backwards. With the stretcher right there, it should be a snap. I don't see anything broken, 'cept his nose, so hopefully, no problem."

Moving like the well-rehearsed team they are, the two men have the teen out of the car and ready for transport just as the Ambulance crew walk in. "Great timing guys." says Davis as the cute girl from station 2 walks up. "Or should I say guy and gal. We've just extracted number 1, and won't have number 2 ready for a while yet. Why don't you do the quick transpo, and we'll wait here. Sarge is wedged in over there, and I don't think we can get him out right now."

"Not a problem," smiled the girl, "we were 45 minutes from dinner, this way we may make it back in time. Lets get him loaded and we can go over the paperwork."

The LT was near the front of the car with one of the rescue struts. Green and Brown each had one of the big inflatable bags. The bags are slipped between the undercarriage of the car and the desk. There isn't much space, but when the rear tires had been deflated, the bottom lifted a few inches. Every little bit helped.

With the bags in place and hooked up, they are inflated as quickly as is safe. Once the car is off the desk, the struts are put in place to support the weight of the car, and the bags deflated and removed. The whole procedure takes 7 minutes.

Now, very slowly, the men push the desk out from under the car, and away from Jade, Just a little bit at first, so Sarge can get close enough to support her, and get the collar on her neck. Then enough to get the back board in and secure her to it. Finally, they are able to lay her flat, start a line and get the heart monitors in place. Once they are sure she is stable enough to transport, Jade is onto the gurney, into the rig and off they go to AAMC.

Alice is giving Davis answers to as many of the questions on his form as she can. Jake is going to meet them at the hospital. Sarge said she can ride with them in the ambulance, up front. She can't believe it has only been 23 minutes since she heard the crash.

Sarge monitors Jade's vitals, Stevens watches the IV, and Davis drives. She is breathing and has a pulse; both are miracles at this point. Sarge runs his hands over her arms and legs, noting the pain reaction to her left radius, and her left ankle. He debates taking off her boot, but looks up and realizes that they have arrived. As they pull into Anne Arundal Medical Center, Jade begins to moan.

"You're doing just fine," Sarge says. "We're at the hospital now. The doctor's will be treating you any minute. Just hang on for a few minutes longer." She's out again before he's done speaking.

Two ER residents opened the rear doors before the brake is even set. The crew dismounted and removed the stretcher in a well-known dance. Sarge is reading off the stats, as they wheel Jade into the trauma room.

"30 year old female, auto drove through store front and landed on her desk, pinning her. Pulse weak and thready, breathing shallow, rales noticeable. Unconscious on scene, started moaning as we pulled up. No obvious external injuries, possible broken left arm, not displaced. Left ankle appears swollen, with boots on, hard to tell; noticed it as we were pulling in, figured you'd see to it."

Both men help the nurses and doctor transfer Jade to the trauma bed. Sarge pulls their gurney from the room and walks to the desk to fill out paperwork. Not the best part of the job. For every 15 minutes of rescue work, it seems like there is an hour of paperwork. Between the hospital and the station, he feels like a damn secretary. Some days he really looks forward to retirement.

Stevens stood in the corner of trauma room 3. He is waiting for the backboard, officially. But he really wants to see how she is. The doctor shouted out orders for portable X-rays, CAT scans, blood work-ups, IV's, etc. Everything you expect him to do in a case like this.

The staff cut off the rest of her clothes, remove her boots. Stevens turns his head until she is covered again. It's not that he hasn't seen a lot of naked women on the job, but when you are in the middle of it, you don't register it as a pretty woman. You are looking for breaks and lacerations or putting on monitors, running IV's. They aren't breasts or thighs, or whatever. Jade is a very pretty woman, and he isn't working this trauma anymore, so he is a gentleman.

Machines are wheeled in and tests are run. Blood is taken; IV's are hung, meds added, notes taken. Every step is called out in a ritual of medical ballet. "Blood pressure is dropping...internal bleeding, no known cause. liver? spleen? kidneys? Phone the OR; tell them we're on our way. Is anyone here to sign? Someone came in with her, in the waiting room. Randall get the forms signed. George we need two more whole units, typed and cross matched..."

In the waiting room, Intern Jessica (Jessie) Randall calls for the family of Jade Worth. Jake has just arrived as Alice stands up. They both rush toward her as she leads them to a small conference room.

"How's Jade? Is she alive?" Jake demands.

"She's loosing a lot of blood; it looks like liver or spleen damage, possibly other organs. We need permission to do surgery."

"Of course...anything. Where do I sign? I'm her husband."
"Right here. This is for an exploratory, as we don't know what we'll find, or what we'll need." Jessie hands Jake the forms and a pen, showing him where to sign.

Alice just sits there sniffling quietly as she watches the two of them. "It's all my fault," she thinks. "If I hadn't asked Jade to come in today. If I hadn't been so afraid of being alone and having people angry about having to wait, or losing business, she could have been home where she belonged on her birthday."

"I'll have a nurse take you up to the OR waiting room as soon as I get these to the surgeon." Jessie states.

"Wait, before you go, I'm A+," Jake says. "If Jade needs blood, I'll make a direct donation. I know as her husband I can do that."

"I'm A+ too," Alice adds, feeling better that she might be able to help after all.

Jessie leaves in a hurry as Jake and Alice walk back into the general waiting room. Finding two chairs next to each other they sit down.
"
Tell me again what happened? Jake asks. "It was so hard to understand you on the phone. You said something about a horse, attacking her."

Alice begins to recount the events of the last 45 minutes in a much calmer, clearer manner. Just as she is finishing up, a nurse comes and leads them to the waiting room near the third floor-operating suite. There the two people closest to Jade try to support each other as they wait for news.

In the OR, the surgeon makes a 6" incision from an inch below the xiphoid bone, where the end of Jade's ribs came together, past her navel, down to her Caesarian-scar. Spreading the incision carefully, Doctor Rook delicately palpates the organs most often associated with silent hemorrhage after blunt trauma. Starting with the liver, he conducts a quick assessment of the vital organs.

"Liver, right lobe, needs resection," he starts reading off the damage for the room recorder. "Spleen; Intestines; bowel; stomach; pancreas; left kidney all intact. Get clamps on the superior hepatic artery. More drainage here, and be sure we're capturing as much blood as we can to recycle." The head nurse assures him they were.

Gently lifting the liver, he sees the right kidney is irreparably damaged and the gall bladder is torn. This is going to be a real

197

Bitch! Turning to his resident, Graves, he tells her to check if any of the renal surgeons are in the building. He needs a second surgeon, STAT!

Rook looks up as Graves hangs up the phone. "I'm sorry Doctor, the On Call is in surgery, and won't be available for at least 3 hours. No one on the renal staff is around. Do you want me to have someone called in?"

"No, Graves," he says, "She can't wait that long. We'll just have to do it. See if you can find me a Sr. Resident or Attending, I need some experience here. Now!"

He turns back to Jade to stop the bleeding. Rook quickly clamps the hepatic artery, and the portal and central veins to the damaged lobe. That slows the bleeding around the liver.

The kidney is the primary problem and has to come out first, but moving the liver aside to clear the field created a challenge. It's so fragile, it can easily rupture, yet the process of making the common bile duct, and rerouting main veins and artery is very time consuming. There doesn't seem to be another way.

Just as he has Graves move beside him, to hold the abdominal retractor he has managed to move the liver onto, the doors open and Dr. Jerome enters. "Damn I'm glad to see you! This is a mess," says Rook with a sigh.

"Sorry to take so long, I was in ER, checking out a hit by car. Don't know why they called me he'll be fine. Just a broken leg, needs ortho, not me! What's going on here?" Jerome asks as he took his place opposite Rook.

As Dr. Rook gives him the run down, Dr. Jerome does a quick assessment, and agrees with the current plan of operation. With Jerome's general surgery experience and Rook's trauma surgery specialty, they know have a fighting chance of saving their patient.

With Graves holding the shifted liver, the two doctors get to work releasing the kidney. They clamp the renal vein and artery to be sure the bleeding is under control. Once they have a dry bed, they tie off both vessels on each side of the clamps, and release them to be sure the bleeding has stopped. When they are sure this will hold, they cut the artery and the vein with a laser knife, which cauterizes the vessel, sealing it as well.

Next, they close the right ureter in the same manner, sealing off its blood supply as they go. Last is all the connective tissue and they remove the kidney to a disposal basin. Through out this procedure, the "Gas Passer" Dr. Roberts, the anesthesiologist, is calling out blood pressure numbers, and other vital statistics, so the two surgeons know the stability of their patient.

Once the kidney is removed, the gall bladder is next and easy, as the right half of the liver is being removed anyway. If they were only removing the gall bladder, the doctors would have to worry about damage to the common bile duct. As they will be creating a new one, this isn't a consideration this time.

Now it's time to do the liver resection. There are eight branches of the hepatic artery, and they need to cut four. The portal and central veins will need to be rerouted to the left lobe, and a new bile duct created into the small intestine, so Jade can digest her food. All slow, precise, procedures, normally done by micro-surgeons. Neither Rook nor Jerome was trained in this specialty. They will have to do things the more archaic style of the pre-micro revolution in medicine.

They really don't think the patient is going to worry about the scar, but they are worried about everything holding together. The damage is so extensive, it seems one good sneeze and she'll just fall apart.

At least they had the laser scalpels; the instant cautery is a blessing. While Rook worked on the bile duct, Jerome worked on the veins and arteries. The two doctors are keeping a close ear out, as Jade's vitals remain very low and uneven. Just as Dr. Rook is making the incision into the left lobe of her liver, to attach the artificial tubing that will pass the bile between the liver and the small intestine, Jade flat-lines.

Dr. Roberts calls out her numbers; Dr. Rook starts ordering meds from the nurses; Dr Jerome starts heart compressions until the crash cart is brought to the table and hooked up...

"Charge to 100," yells Rook, "Clear!" as he applies the paddles. No effect, "200...Clear!" again, no effect, "250...Clear!"

Jade is looking down on the frantic scene in the operating room. That is her dying there on the table. Shouldn't she care or something? Don't you have emotions when you are dead? Guess not! She sees a great light, off in the distance, and feels compelled to move go towards it.

Suddenly the three women are in her way. "Stop!" they shout. "It's too soon. You have to break the curse, you have to go back, it's the only way."

"I have a choice?" she asks, very surprised. She looks pretty dead to her.

"Yes." Says Lilac Wolf, "your medicine can save you, but you must want to be saved. I didn't know, so I didn't want. You must want."

"She's right Jade," added Jeanette, "We never had the chance, but we'd have all fought like the dickens to stay with our families if we could have. It's up to you to fight for all of us now."

"Yah, meine Liebchen. Your family needs you. I do remember you as a kinder; you would come and sit to read to me. I was a very old woman and the other children, they all played, but you would always bring the book, and read to me. You said the adults were boring, and the children were too rough, we'd be "the ladies" and read. So now, listen to me, as I used to listen to you. Go back to your little ones, back to your handsome husband. Go back, and save us all."

"How, how do I do it? The pull is so strong."

"Stronger than a mother's love? Than a granddaughter's patience? Just remember your love for your family, remember all the people who love you and need you still. Remember that we are your family, and we love you and need you too. Go back Leibling, go back."

Even as she says it, Jade is returning to her body, she hears the doctor say "350 again...Clear! And just begins to hear a beep as she goes under again.

The room erupts into cheers as the monitor beeps. "I've got pulse and pressure," calls Roberts. "She's back!"

"That's great, thanks everyone for your help, now let's see that she makes it through the rest of this operation." Rook replies.

"Amen to that!" comes from Jerome, and the two men get back to the job at hand.

When Jake is finally let into Jade's room, it's a little after nine that night. She makes it through the rest of the surgery, and out of recovery, but still isn't conscious. The doctors say she can wake up any minute, or may stay in this light coma for days. There hasn't been any brain swelling, or damage that they can see, but it's possible the accident caused enough of a shake to produce local swelling that might not show up for a few days.

Looking at Jade in the hospital bed, with all these tubes and things running in and out of her, he is beside himself in grief. He feels so helpless. There isn't anything he can do to help her. All this Beware 30 stuff, he keeps thinking, those dreams, the horses, and here she's almost killed by a mustang. I just don't get it. What's going on? Is she the next? She lived; does that mean the curse is broken? Is she safe now?

"I should have been there damn it! I should have saved her." He says, aloud. "I'll never leave you alone again." He promises her, laying his head down on the side of the bed and crying.

"Mmm, ok," Jade, mumbles groggily. Jake snaps his head up and there was Jade smiling weakly at him. "Hello there mister." She says.

"You're awake; they said it might take days." Jake babbles. "How are you, how do you feel?"

201

"Like I was hit by a car," Jade tries to joke. But it falls rather flat. "I'm pretty drugged up at the moment. It's a good thing they have me anchored with all these tubes and things, or I think I'd be scraping the ceiling. So just, what happened? I mean I know about the car, and I know I lived. I can see the bandages, the cast. I know I had surgery. How bad? Am I missing any legs? Or anything else important?"

"No limbs, part of your liver, right kidney, and gall bladder. Two cracked ribs on the lower right side. Broken left arm, just a slight fracture really, not a big deal considering. And your left ankle is sprained.

All things considered, you're going to be in great shape. They almost lost you on the table, as they were working on your liver, but managed to bring you back…and here you are."

"Yeah, I know about the episode in the middle of the surgery. I was aware then. You know all those stories you've heard about. People saying they had out-of-body experiences. Well I guess I'm one of them now. I was up in the corner of the operating room, watching them try to revive me, when I felt this strong urge to float in a certain direction. There really is a light. Bright doesn't do it justice. It's the most beautiful thing I've ever seen. There are all the colors possible in this light, and as bright as it is, it doesn't hurt your eyes. You just know it is total love.

As I was happily drifting towards it, the three ancestors ambushed me. That's the only thing I can call it. One second I'm drifting into eternal peace, the next they are between it and me. They told me that I had to come back. Back to you and the kids. That's how I was to break the curse. To have my love of family be stronger than my love of self. It would have been so easy to just keep going. The pull is so strong.

Then the grandmothers started reminding me about how much you and the kids needed me. About how much I would miss you, how much I wanted to watch the kids grow up in person. How much I didn't want to become them.

As I was floating back into my body, they were saying

'Beware 30...must warn the next!'

Now I can say ...

...Life begins at 30!"

The End!

www.ingramcontent.com/pod-product-compliance
Lightning Source LLC
Chambersburg PA
CBHW020603250626
47154CB00004B/1338